The Sacrificial Deal

Teri Harmon

Copyright© 2020 by Teri Harmon

All rights reserved. Published in the United States by Polyverse Publications LLC, Santa Barbara.

www.polyversepublications.com

Polyverse Publications and the colophon are trademarks of Polyverse Publications, LLC.

Book and cover design by Louis F. Torres

Library of Congress Control Number: pending

ISBN: 978-1-7378832-3-4 (paperback)

Printed in the United States of America

1 2 3 4 5 6 7 8 9 10

First Edition

I cannot confirm whether this story is true or not – so don't ask me!

Chapter 1

The public knows little about modern-day crime families. The fact that they exist and control vast empires of wealth is often secret with various technologies giving them the ability to cover up their trails of lies, deceit, cheating, and dirty business dealings with ease. They walk among us and look like our neighbors, but beneath it all, they operate in their own world with their own set of rules. Get in their way or find yourself in the wrong place at the wrong time, and you are in big trouble.

One so-called 'family' in Santa Barbara was entrenched in many businesses, mostly legitimate, to help cover up for those that were not. Many would be surprised to learn who their golfing buddy really is, or their grocer, or restaurateur, or even their own doctor! These people could blend in anywhere, increasing their wealth at someone else's expense. This Mafioso-style family, known as the Kozlovs, migrated from Russia in the 1980s, bringing with them their nefarious flare for illegal activities, including pharmaceutical connections for their extremely competitive and growing drug empire. If you were unfortunate enough to cross them or cause them trouble, you might go missing and never be heard from again.

It was late at night and the brothers Pavel and Andrei Kozlov were agitated — yelling back and forth over a glass of their favorite alcoholic beverage — from across the black matching sofas at Pavel's home. They had gotten angry about a pharmaceutical rep known only as "Carson" that had not delivered the supplies to their warehouse when he promised he would. One excuse for such tardiness could be accepted, but the repeated excuses and increasing carelessness in which the rep had communicated hadn't given the Kozlov brothers any faith in a future delivery. A large sum of money had been fronted to Carson who probably blew it all gambling and lavish spending per the word on the street. This had two effects on the business of dealing in illegal drugs...

1) if the competition found out the Kozlovs were stiffed and didn't retaliate, the same thing could happen again with someone else.

2) They were out the $500,000 deposit but could have turned that inventory into over $10 million by the time the supplies were converted to a saleable product on the street. The Kozlov's considered this a loss of $10 million, not just the $500,000 originally paid to the greedy Carson.

"Pavel, I'm tired of waiting and the excuses…. Carson needs to be seriously confronted… now. We're going to need Oleg's help – let's make the call and confront this piss ant tomorrow night," said Andrei whose veins were popping out of his neck as he struggled to control his anger.

Pavel agreed with his brother and made the fateful call to Oleg to set in motion what could not be stopped.

"Oleg, this has gone on long enough – it's time to deal with Carson. Set it up for a late-night meeting at his office. No witnesses. You know the rest – got it?"

The only response Pavel heard from Oleg was "got it."

The Kozlovs were trying to set up one of their biggest drug deals to date and would see it through to its completion, no matter what the obstacle or cost.

Chapter 2

Sarah didn't need an alarm clock because her 7-year-old golden retriever put his wet nose on her cheek every morning at exactly 6:30.

"Aw, Max, your breath!" said Sarah, slowly waking and sitting up in bed.

"Go wake daddy." Max trotted to the other side of the bed and stuck his nose into Nicholas's face. Nicholas groaned and pulled the covers over his head in an ill-fated attempt to gain a few more minutes of peace before the busy day began.

"Up, up," Sarah said as she moved to curl up next to Nicholas for a brief second. Nicholas rolled toward her to plant his obligatory morning kiss on his wife and moaned "Can't Max ever wake Susan up first?" wrapping his arms around Sarah as she tried to get out of bed.

"Stay," he half-jokingly said to her.

In all the years of their marriage, their

predictable morning routine had changed little and was comfortable for them both. Sarah and Nicholas had met in college and married when Sarah was twenty-one, unintentionally starting a family almost immediately. Sarah went on to med school, navigating both motherhood and school as if it were the norm for all women of her time to do – which it wasn't. She was extremely organized and thrived on the demands of trying to make it all work. Nicholas had earned his master's degree in architecture and worked for a large firm not far from where they lived in Santa Barbara.

Twenty-five years later and Dr. Sarah Stevens was a respected pediatrician, Nicholas an established architect. Their first-born, Sophie, now twenty-five, was a tall, lanky kindergarten teacher who loved to play beach volleyball. With her sandy blond hair and easygoing disposition, she looked the part of a beach town resident. Sophie met her husband, Austin O'Neill, during college and thought he looked like a young version of the actor Robin Williams. Sophie and Austin married the year before and lived in the neighboring town of Goleta not far from Sophie's parents.

Their second child, Jackson, now twenty-one,

was a junior at the University of California, Santa Barbara, and lived off-campus a couple of miles from home with his buddies. He looked a lot like his dad with wavy dark brown hair and a conservative flare for wearing button-down shirts and bow ties when dating the local coeds.

Their youngest, Susan, eighteen, was a senior in high school and the only one of the three Stevens kids considering a career in medicine... as a veterinarian.

Nicholas and Sarah considered Max their last baby, and both felt lucky and blessed to have their close-knit family all living relatively near them and thriving within their own worlds.

Sarah went through her days meticulously taking care of everyone but herself. She gave her all to family and career but paid no attention to those little things in life that would give her the giggles, belly laughs, or just some time to reflect on her surroundings to smell the proverbial roses. Her busy lifestyle was routine bound and kept her moving forward, but it had also added pounds to her once slender and athletic build. Sarah didn't have the time or energy to do the serious workouts she should have prescribed for herself. Walking Max between her office and hospital was all she could fit into her busy lifestyle.

Fortunately, and thanks to her helpful business partner Dr. Kathy, Sarah had made time over the years to participate in her kids' activities. She loved helping with scouting projects and being assistant room mom for her kids' classrooms. Weekends brought with them carpool trips to various sporting activities, charitable work for the hospital, and annual birthday parties for the family. The Stevens children were kept busy and thereby out of trouble – most of the time.

From behind the scenes was Claire, a wonderful housekeeper who had been with them since they moved into the neighborhood years prior. Her twice-a-week help took some of the pressure off the busy parents with daily household tasks. Despite this luxury, the Stevens kids were still expected to clean their rooms, do chores, and learn how to be responsible for their own space—another set of non-negotiable routines that were to be followed.

Sarah kissed Nicholas and climbed over him to get out of bed as Max went out the bedroom door to wake up Susan with his wet nose – as was his doggy duty to do so. In the kitchen, the morning energy picked up with the family all individually trying to eat their breakfast concoctions, make lunches, check the day's schedule, and get out the door on time.

Sarah didn't like to cook so that task was delegated to Nicholas who claimed he enjoyed cooking or at least jokingly stated that "he had to – to survive." Ordering from the various restaurants in the area able to deliver or had pick-up was a popular option for the Stevens family.

"Who wants toast?" Nicholas asked while toasting his favorite sourdough bread.

"Not me, dad, and FYI, I'll be home late – I'm studying for midterms with Abby. She invited me to stay for dinner," Susan said in between her bites of eggs and sausage. Susan took her schooling seriously and was dedicated to becoming a veterinarian.

"I also have track after school." Susan's build was a lot like her older sister's which gave her the edge over the competition on the track. With her auburn hair pulled back tight, long legs, and an athletic build – she was easily recognizable on the track and tough to beat. Waving a form around Susan stated, "Oh, and I need one of you to sign this permission slip for tomorrow's track meet, it's an away game and we're taking the bus again."

Nicholas silently reached out for the form to sign while munching on his breakfast and asked "Hon… how about you… toast? And Susan, chores done?"

Susan grabbed the signed form and proudly declared "chores done."

Sarah's mind was already in motion organizing her day while she packed leftovers from the night before for lunch, all while quickly drinking her daily protein shake.

"I'll pass on the toast as well — Susan do you need a ride to school or are you carpooling with Abby again — and please don't give Max a sausage!" Sarah pleaded just as Susan was about to share a link with the beloved family dog.

Sarah continued to keep the day organized and expectations in line. "Nic, Jackson is going to pick up Max today, so my guess is both are going to be home in time for dinner."

"OK… see you all later… I'm off to design a

10

masterpiece. I'll bring home some dinner, but I may also be a tad bit late as I'm meeting with a new client and not sure how long that's going to take." Nicholas finished his toast and grabbed his overstuffed briefcase while heading toward the garage.

After waking up his family and doing his business outside, Max had his own routine that if lucky — included a forbidden sausage from Susan, while listening to the garbled conversations of his people pack, and then going to the office with Sarah to console the young patients. Max observed the Stevens as they finished their morning rituals, and all left in different cars.

He rode with Sarah - who was unaware that her routine would soon collide with an unscripted destiny.

Chapter 3

Sarah's partner in her private practice was her best friend, Dr. Kathy Mitchell. They had first met in med school while dissecting a cadaver together. Multiple times the pregnant Sarah had almost passed out from the overwhelming stench of the formaldehyde and had to make a run for the bathroom to avoid throwing up in front of her classmates. Once Kathy discovered Sarah was pregnant, and not just being wimpy, they laughed the incidents off and quickly became study buddies and supportive best friends throughout med school. Both women were there for the births of each other's babies and named each other as godmothers for their first-born children. Kathy's husband Greg and Nicholas became best friends, as did their families, with Nicholas and Greg often joking that they each had two wives.

Sarah and Kathy had a dream of opening their own practice, which became a reality soon after receiving their degrees and finishing their internships. Their practice became one of the busiest pediatric offices in Santa Barbara and was geared toward putting their young clients at ease before they even got inside.

One of Nicholas's favorite projects was to design Sarah and Kathy's new energy-efficient office with environmentally friendly materials and a whimsically decorated glass wall that made their offices visible to the kids arriving from the corridor outside. Sarah and Kathy loved it when their patients waved at them through the window just before entering the cheerful office. The kids also learned how to wave the lights on and thought it was fun flailing their arms about – up and down the halls to do it.

Not long after they first opened their practice, a little boy arriving for an appointment saw Sarah munching on a carrot as he passed by the glass wall with his mom. The little patient eagerly entered Sarah's office laughing...

"Dr. Sarah, you look just like Bugs Bunny," the boy shouted while smiling.

"Yeah," Sarah asked, "you think so? Well then… What's up Doc?" she said leaning in with a big smile. The boy found it so funny that it became a part of their routine whenever he came to see her. Soon, her other little patients picked up on the fun nickname which put them at ease and made her seem more accessible and less threatening.

As the years went on, a collection of patients' drawings and craft projects filled the office walls with color and life — and every so often, a carrot was found on Sarah's desk. When Max came along, he became a welcome fixture, he even had his own hospital-like bed to rest in and patiently endured the affection as the mascot for both the office and in the hospital next door where he and Sarah made their rounds.

As Sarah and Max entered the office, Sarah's mind was occupied with her involvement in the design and implementation of a new pediatric wing for the hospital next door. She and Kathy had recently found out that they were to be the new co-chiefs of pediatrics, which meant they would be intimately involved in the project from start to finish, as well as oversee it upon completion. They had long been concerned about how the hospital could improve on its services to children and even though it would be a long, complicated process, they were intent on developing it into the best pediatric center on the west coast.

Sarah and Kathy had plans for a state-of-the-art research facility that included a very kid-friendly children's ward supported by programs to help children learn about their own care and treatment. All of this would be overseen and delivered by staff members who understood how scary it was for children facing hospitals stays. The new children's wing would be philosophically and physically structured after Sarah and Kathy's current office; compassionate, happy, and welcoming — all the elements that had made their private practice so successful. It was their dream project.

Sarah tossed Max a treat and scanned the appointment book on the receptionist's computer as Kathy came into the office, clapping to trigger the overly efficient lighting system back on.

"Hey, you! Did you see some of the comments from the design committee regarding the fourth floor?" Kathy wasted no time in getting to the point while putting her armful of notebooks and purse down.

"And a good morning to you too. No, I'm

going to review them tonight and yes, I'm staying here late since Nick and Susan will be home late. How do they look?" Sarah responded as she looked up at Kathy.

"Well, most of our input was used but we still need to push back on some of their budget constraints and use of space in the waiting rooms. The bean counters nixed a couple of our requests, but I have it on good authority it's all negotiable," Kathy mentioned while scanning the same appointment book Sarah was reviewing.

"Are you two coming over this weekend? We can BBQ and talk more about the plans — you should know by then what your thoughts are about it and I'd love to get Nick's take on some of the schematics." Glancing at the clock Kathy continued, "It's almost time for lucky patient number one to arrive... I'm going to start reviewing files. You all set for next door?"

"Yep — all set. Where is our PA... late again?" Sarah was always punctual and didn't like anyone to be late for work and scanned the office for signs of their number one assistant. Within seconds of wondering, he arrived winded, attempting to be on time. The two doctors gave their assistant 'the double stare' — one at him and one at the clock, rolled their eyes and started their day — Kathy seeing patients in the office, and Sarah off to the hospital to check on her patients.

"I'll see you later," Sarah said to Kathy who waved without looking up from her appointment book.

"C'mon, Max – you ready to go? We don't want to keep the kids waiting." Sarah knew Max would once again be a hit with her patients, as he had been for his family during their seven years with him. Max was adopted as a puppy and had seen both Sophia and Jackson move away and seemed to miss their lavish attention and treats. Sarah had encountered service dogs in the hospital before and thought that with Max's loveable disposition he would make a great 'healing ambassador' and brought him to work one day to see how he would do, rather than leaving him alone at home. He was an instant hit and loved meeting the patients and receiving their attention, so it was decided he would accompany Sarah most days during her rounds.

"Hello, Christine! How are you today? Max and

I are here to check up on you… how was your breakfast? Did you get pancakes again? How's your shoulder doing? Max, what do you think? I think it's looking better." Max just stared up at the little girl while resting his snout on the bedside while Sarah went about her informal examination of little Christine's shoulder.

"Good thing you were done with breakfast, Max might have tried to talk you into sharing part of it… did you know he likes sausages?" Christine giggled a bit and leaned over with her good arm to pet Max while Sarah finished her examination and reviewed her chart.

"Ok Christine… your shoulder is looking good; I'll talk to your mom and dad about you going home today…. how does that sound? Looking towards Max for confirmation, Sarah added, "I think Max agrees!"

And so, the rounds went, with the dynamic duo of Sarah and Max soothing the kid's nerves while making sure treatments were working, and healing was in motion. On the way back to the office, Sarah was on the phone returning calls while taking a shortcut across a grassy area and stepped in a pile of doggie doo!

"OH CRAP!" She loudly exclaimed and tried to wipe her shoes on the grass to remove it while struggling to keep her composure as she continued talking to a colleague on the cell phone. As the pair rounded the office building's corner, Max saw Jackson and immediately ran to his buddy for his special day with the college boys.

It had been decided that Jackson would stop by and take Max with him once a week, to the beach when he surfed, or just to hang out during homework or until dinner time. Today would be one of those hang-out days with Jackson making sure his favorite dog got fed, even if the rest of the family was out late. Max was going to have a very full day.

"Hey mom, did you just step in dog crap?" Jackson said while smirking at his mom's accident. "Wow… that really smells. I'll bring Max home later… what time will you be home?"

"Hi, honey. Dad and I will both be home late — probably after 7:00. Can you feed Max before you take off… and how's school going?" Sarah was judicious with her words and time but wanted her family to know she would always make time for them.

"It's going… the waves are pretty good right now; I think Jeff and I will hit the beach for an hour then head in for some studying. Don't worry, I'll feed Maxy boy, and I'll pick him up tomorrow as well. One of my classes was canceled so I have most of tomorrow open for studying — can I take him?

"Yes, he'll like hanging out with you, but please try not to get any of that beach tar on his paws… You know it's not easy getting that stuff off! Thanks, honey… gotta run and get *this* crap off. Love you."

Sarah headed back to the office to start her patient appointments, but first put on a pair of what looked like hospital slippers she had hidden in her desk for such accidents. Kathy smirked as she walked past Sarah and noticed the slippers… and heard her signature incredibly loud sneeze usually triggered by the walks back and forth past the hospital's flowering plants. This was not the first time her business partner had stepped in dog poop during her shortcuts back and forth from the hospital!

Sarah was now left on her own to finish up with her patients, attend meetings, and do research that would keep her at the office later than usual. By the time she got home, she found Nicholas asleep in his recliner with the TV on, and the multi-tasker Susan in her room doing homework while talking on the phone. Max was asleep at the foot of Susan's bed, so tired from his busy beach day with the college boys that he could barely wag his tail in greeting. When Susan finally emerged from her room she had a quick chat with her mom about the next day and then managed to give her mom a good night hug, which Sarah treasured. Susan had been great at dispensing hugs up until she hit high school and then stopped for some unknown adolescent reason. But just recently, Susan had decided it was once again okay to hug her parents and had resumed the practice, to the delight of them both.

It looked like leftovers found in the refrigerator would be Sarah's dinner, followed by her usual bedtime routine, which now ended with her reading and writing reports and recommendations for the new pediatric wing until she fell asleep. The medical office and home life routine kept her world predictable and comfortable. Specifically, routines allowed Sarah to balance the demands of her time with the needs of her family taking priority. Little did Sarah know the magnitude of the upcoming disruption that would throw her world and family on its head!

Chapter 4

On Friday morning, Max made his usual rounds to wake up his family. It was going to be a big day for Susan and her friends commemorating their last high school homecoming celebration… and Sarah hoped to be a part of the getting ready festivities. Susan had just outgrown her pre-adolescent awkwardness and had developed an independent streak, insisting that she and her posse get themselves dressed for the big night without parental help, assuring her mom that photos would be taken to record the event. Susan headed off, with the football game and following dance foremost on her mind.

Sarah sighed. "Teenagers!"

Sarah was silently disappointed in not being able to witness her youngest child's final, time-honored high school ritual before leaving the nest for college. It was ok to know she wasn't needed — but she did want to be wanted. To keep her mind off it, the efficient doctor decided she would stay late at work to make progress on the hospital project. Jackson would be picking up Max for the afternoon, so it was the perfect opportunity to close out another busy week. Sarah told Nicholas she would be home late and once again they all left their home in separate cars.

While sitting at her desk that evening, typing away on her keyboard between taking bites of her left-over Chinese take-out lunch, Sarah paused long enough to notice it was just after 10:00 p.m. — time to call it quits for the day. She organized her notes for Kathy's review and started to put her desk in order. Her final task before locking up was to wave her arms to turn on the lights, take some paperwork to the fax machine room at the end of the hall, and send the faxes out.

Within minutes of disappearing into the fax room, three men exited the elevator outside her office suite and entered the office across the hall to pay a visit to the startled pharmaceutical rep inside.

As Sarah hovered over her noisy fax machine, she couldn't hear the loud arguing from across the hall. But as she walked back toward her now-dark office,

Sarah abruptly stopped at the threshold upon hearing three loud bangs just feet from where she was standing, shielded only by glass and the dark hallway. Her attention was immediately drawn to the three men standing on the other side of the glass wall and saw what looked like a fourth man wriggling in pain on the floor in front of them. In that split moment, Sarah regretted the transparency her glass wall provided and hoped it wouldn't reveal her whereabouts to these angry-looking men.

There are guns in their hands! Sarah thought frantically. A more deliberate glance revealed the fourth man was lying in a growing pool of blood. As she stood speechless and horrified at the scene — the newly faxed papers dropped from her hands. One of the papers fell into her office triggering those damn energy-efficient lights back on.

As if conducted by the office light to do so, all three men whipped around in unison to see where and why the light had come on. A wave of terror washed over her as she was exposed — standing in full view of the crime they had just committed. In particular, she saw the dark hollow eyes and bald head of what appeared to be the head shooter glaring at her. Illuminated by the hallway lights there was no way to hide what these men had just done with the body of evidence at their feet. Illuminated behind the glass wall there was nowhere for Sarah to hide from what she had just seen. In what seemed like an eternity, but was just seconds, they all stared at each other in utter shock and disbelief with their circumstances. The men knew there was a witness who saw them commit murder, and intuitively knew they had to immediately get rid of her. It was late at night — no one would see a second shooting — and they were angry at being caught. They now had their guns pointed right at Sarah, all they had to do was to stop thinking about this unexpected twist of fate and pull the trigger.

After unbelievingly staring at the murderous men, Sarah realized the gravity of the moment that included guns now pointed at her. Adrenaline surged through her veins, and Sarah gasped instinctively sprinting for the emergency exit at the back of her office. One of the men extended his arm and took aim — firing at the fleeing figure. Fortunately for her, the gunman missed his moving target, but the glass walls shattered, affording the shooter a quick way to go in after her while the triggered security alarms howled in protest.

Sarah knew her way around the building and all its exits. She quickly ran out of the closest door which led out to an area of the building's grounds that fortunately had adequate shrubbery to hide behind. If she ran out in the open, she could be shot. Sarah dove into the bushes while holding her breath, hoping that she wasn't followed and wouldn't be found. Patting herself down, she realized she had nothing to defend herself with other than her stethoscope. She frantically looked around and silently prayed that the blaring sound of the alarms would scare off the shooters. Moments later, she heard tires squealing loudly.

Sarah cautiously peeked out of the bushes and was relieved to see what looked like a dark-colored Mercedes sedan speeding out of the parking structure and heading down the street. It was too loud and fast for an innocent to be doing at this time of night — it had to be 'them'.

Still trembling and not sure what she should do, Sarah suddenly remembered the man who had been shot. As if on automatic pilot, Sarah went back in for her medical bag to revisit the terrifying scene and offer help to the victim if not already dead.

Sarah recognized the semi-conscience man as the one who had called on her office numerous times representing his employer's pharmaceutical products. He had seemed friendly but was never the type she would do business with. There was just something about him that bugged her, but at this point, none of that mattered. He had been shot what looked like two or three times in the chest and arm and was profusely bleeding and fading fast.

Though barely conscious, the man recognized Sarah and mumbled something that sounded like, "They know who you are. Not safe!" He tried to repeat himself several times, but the words came out slow and garbled. Sarah grabbed gauze, tourniquets, and other items from her medical bag with one hand while she applied pressure on two of the wounds to stop his bleeding with the other. Sarah worked fast and knew the hospital was literally across the street but her efforts at that moment were more important in stabilizing him.

No time to call. Keep working on him, Sarah thought. Despite her quick and efficient efforts to save his life, Carson took his last, labored breath and died.

Sarah sat down, looked around at the bloody corridor sprinkled with the shattered glass from her office wall, put her head into her hands, and began to cry. As the shock translated to unexpected sobs, the alarm system's protocols worked to bring the police. They arrived to find Sarah dazed with blood on her hands from trying to revive Carson. She could barely talk or put into words what she had witnessed - she felt numb and confused over the quickness in which it all happened. Many questions were asked by the police who were feverishly taking notes and calling for the coroner and additional help. She put her arm up to point at the security cameras and mumbled to call the security company to review what their cameras had captured... and numbly repeated her recount several times to make sure the police officers present could confirm what had happened. The officer that asked the most questions seemed to be in charge, finally informed Sarah of their next steps.

"Dr. Stevens, we need to take you to our

station for further questioning and to help us to recon-
struct the events of tonight for our reports — you can
ride in my car." Sarah complied and during the drive
heard the officer call in to have the station ready to receive her. Behind the scenes, officers were already in
contact with the security company to obtain the recording devices and were ready to review them despite
the late hour. Things were happening fast and all she
could think of - to ask for - was when she could call
her husband.

"Sir, I'm not feeling very well and tired. Do we
have to do all this tonight and if so, how long do you
think it will take? "Sarah asked hoping she could go
home and wake up the next day with the whole thing
just a bad nightmare.

The officer replied. "Dr. Stevens, we need to
get your account of the night's events now before you
forget them given the stress this has caused you. We'll
try our best to get it all settled as quickly as we can."
Sarah stared out the window of the police car numb to
her surroundings and wondering what would happen
next.

Chapter 5

Sarah was in shock. The world as she knew it had been turned upside down! Instead of feeling like a competent medical doctor, and given what she had just witnessed, she now felt like a victim. It was an unfamiliar role. She felt nauseous as the detectives surrounded her with questions and comments while they viewed her blood-stained clothes and hands. They had even asked if she wanted an attorney present, which really confused her since she was the witness, not the 'murderer'! As she sat in a room closed off from the rest of the station, people wearing uniforms kept entering and exiting, some asking questions, others taking notes and looking concerned as they heard Sarah recount the events with her eyes closed to help her concentrate and visualize.

Her eyes were wide open, however, as she inspected each mug shot brought to her by a detective. Sarah wondered briefly as to how they were able to bring photos so quickly for review, and then her heart skipped a beat. One of the officers pushed a photo across the desk that made her cringe when she recognized the same hollow eyes paired with the bald head she had seen earlier that evening. Sitting back in her chair and looking at the photo once again to be sure, she took a deep breath and declared, "This looks like one of the men I saw tonight."

"Are you sure?" the detective quizzed her. "It was late and it all happened so fast."

"Positive!" Sarah replied as she pointed to his photo, "What stands out is how ugly he was and his brief stare at me… it was cold and angry looking — just like this mug shot." Sarah quickly remembered that man was closest to her office wall and seemed to be the main shooter — and when she had focused on him — he had looked elated by his deed while the other two men had started to argue.

The concerned detective took a deep breath and sternly said, "Please wait here, and don't talk to anyone about tonight's events," and then promptly left Sarah sitting by herself in the sterile-looking room. The hairs on Sarah's arms went up. Something more was wrong with her situation — the detective outside the door told someone to get the security company's number and then she heard directions to call the police chief and to get him in ASAP. Sarah called out "Sir, could you please tell me who this man is that I pointed out? I'd really like to know — is something wrong with me knowing? When can I go home? Sir?" She didn't know it yet, but Sarah had just identified Oleg – the Kozlov's number one 'associate'.

Chapter 6

Back at home, Nicholas had been comfortably asleep in his favorite chair when he heard the phone ring. He groggily answered it expecting it was Sarah on why she was getting home so late, but immediately jumped up at hearing the words "police station" from the caller. Bewildered and confused as to why his wife was at the local police station, Nicholas anxiously wrote out a quick note for Susan who was due home any minute from the dance, and left for the police station.

Upon arrival, he was told to wait in the lobby for what seemed like an eternity, which caused more frustration at not knowing what had happened to Sarah. Unable to relax or sit down, Nicholas paced up and down the halls worrying about his wife.

Police Chief Garrison entered the private questioning room that Sarah was sitting in and closed the door behind him. The chief had been with this police department for over twenty years and looked the part with his short hair, large frame, and authoritative manner in how he introduced himself. After turning on the recording device sitting on the table, the chief asked Sarah to repeat once again what she had witnessed. He heard her vivid, crisp description retold in detail as she closed her eyes and spoke with full control of her emotions, though she looked exhausted. The chief tried to throw her off by questioning her account to make sure her answers were in line with her previous statements made to his detectives, but she remained consistent. He cautiously turned the pages of mug shots to help her ID the other men, knowing which pages might get a reaction after reviewing the security footage to see for himself who the assailants were.

Sarah had already identified Oleg but was not 100% sure about the other two until the Chief pushed the forty-third and forty-fourth photo in front of her. Sarah's pulse quickened at the familiarity of their cold faces. Sarah didn't know at that moment, but she had just identified the other two men involved in the murder, who had then tried to kill her. To Chief Garrison, Sarah was a credible witness and had incredible composure during the questioning, but Sarah was exhausted from the whole ordeal.

"May I please see my husband now?" she wearily asked the chief.

"There's still a lot of work to be done to get you out of the station, given the sensitive nature of the evening's events," he replied. "Dr. Stevens – Please do NOT talk to anyone else about this case without my presence, not even your husband, until we can get this coordinated with the proper authorities – do you understand what I just said?"

Sarah quickly agreed to the Chief's demands. She would have agreed to anything if it meant a distraction from her present reality and a reunion with her husband. As Nicholas entered the room, Sarah immediately stood up to go hug him. Nicholas was perplexed as to what had happened to his wife and wanted to ask her many questions but was told he couldn't by the Chief as a condition of seeing her. Chief Garrison told Nicholas to "be there" for her. Nicholas was alarmed at the sight of the bloodstains on Sarah's clothes but knew the cause must have been related to whatever had just happened, and besides, she was a doctor.

"Sarah!! Are you okay!? What is happening?" he lovingly asked with a hint of major concern while holding his wife and rubbing her back.

"Yeah, I just need to take a deep breath and clear my mind. I'm starting to get a major headache," she authoritatively replied. Reaching for her purse which she had barely grabbed before being escorted off by the police, Sarah rummaged for something to relieve her pain. The two of them huddled together, spoke a few words, and managed to calm each other by just being together while sequestered in the sterile-looking holding room.

About an hour and two cups of decaf coffee later, two other men came into the questioning room and introduced themselves as FBI agents, which gave Sarah a chill. She immediately knew something awful was about to be shared but didn't know the extent of the trouble she was in, holding Nic's hand tightly for comfort. The FBI agents took turns breaking the proverbial ice explaining who they were before divulging that the gunmen were believed to be the Kozlov brothers. They explained about the brothers' roles within a Russian mob family domiciled in Santa Barbara, which seemed hell-bent on making its mark in the drug world by any means necessary.

"Oh no," Sarah muttered with tears starting down her cheeks — "NO, this can't be happening."

"Oh Crap... is this for real... are you sure these were the men?" Nicholas added.

"Dr. Stevens, Mr. Stevens — I know all of this is hard to comprehend, especially at this late hour, but we need to complete our questioning while you are here and then proceed to put you and your family in protective custody."

As the two agents continued to fill in the blanks about the Kozlovs, the severity of the situation began to sink in for Sarah. She felt nauseated and asked for a restroom, where she heaved up the leftover Chinese food she had for dinner. Afterward, she blotted cold water on her face for minimal relief, her legs still wobbly as she reluctantly exited the bathroom. She walked slowly with an assigned policewoman at her side to help her, but also to keep an eye on Sarah's return to the holding room.

Chief Garrison walked in behind Sarah and dismissed the escort to return to her desk while all involved continued to inform Sarah and Nicholas about the events and the criminal history of the suspects.

"The FBI has been tracking these Russian mobsters for years," said the taller of the two agents. "This group has been involved with a lot of money laundering businesses that were set up and run in such a way as to avoid various agencies being able to track them, or even know which businesses were legitimate or not. Bottom line, Dr. Stevens, you witnessed a murder, which means with your help we could get the most important members of this crime family behind bars forever!"

Chief Garrison noticed the tears welling up in Sarah's eyes and knew she was unprepared to hear the complications surrounding her predicament, but allowed the agents to continue their briefing.

"Usually such higher-ups are never caught doing their own dirty work," his partner explained. "But in this case, the two Kozlov brothers, Pavel and Andrei, were present, along with Oleg Sokotov, one of their head 'associates'. Oleg would normally be the one to carry out the dirty work as previously reported by our intelligence. The Kozlov crime family has been known to conduct horrific acts of violence against those who don't deliver on their promises or interfere with the family's business interests. Something big must have gone down that caused the Kozlovs to be out in person. You saw them, and unfortunately, they saw you!"

Sarah felt screwed as her mind raced in a hundred different directions trying to process it all. Nicholas spoke up —

"So, Mr. Garrison, what are our options here… what can we do? I think we're a bit in shock over the whole thing."

Looking directly at Sarah, Chief Garrison delivered the worst news of the night. "You'll need to testify. We already have agents securing arrest warrants and on their way to apprehend the Kozlovs. You would be the key witness to cripple this crime-ridden family once and for all."

When Sarah heard the fateful word, "testify," her stomach churned.

"Are you serious?" Nicholas yelled. "If these people are as vindictive as you say they are, my wife and our entire family could be at risk! Isn't there another way to deal with this — besides putting my family at risk of becoming victims???"

"Mr. Stevens, these people know who your wife is," one of the agents explained "She is the one person that could put them away."

"You can do your civic duty by going on the offensive to put these wise guys away for good OR be on the defense, looking over your shoulder every day, wondering if your family will ever be safe. We can protect you now and can discuss putting your family in the Witness Protection Program. We can also fast-track your case and have a trial date in less than one month, given these unique circumstances."

Sarah felt like throwing up again. "I thought court cases could take years before being heard," she wearily remarked. The FBI agents went into detail about expedited case disposition and special circumstances when it came to organized crime that could be applied in this instance to compel a judge to fast track their case.

"But first and foremost," the second agent urged, "is the importance and need for everyone's safety. It won't take long for the Kozlovs to find out where you live. Time is of the essence! Mr. Stevens, call your kids and tell them to start packing enough clothes for two weeks and to do it in less than thirty minutes… just toss clothes in a large trash bag, no fancy time-consuming packing. Tell them some police officers will be by any minute to collect them. Mr. Stevens, I would recommend we go get your youngest daughter first, who you said is at home. Our agents can pick up the others, you can call them on the way, but we need to get your youngest daughter *now*."

The agent then turned to Sarah. "Dr. Stevens, we'll need you to remain in this room for the time being. When everyone has been assembled here — you will be transported to a safe house to get some sleep."

Once Sarah heard the words about her family being in danger, she could no longer keep the floodgate of emotions in check and began to sob as she worried about everyone's fate and asked for a box of tissues. A few minutes later her instincts kicked in as she began asking about the details of assembling her family.

Sarah appreciated that Nicholas was handling the arrangements and communications with the kids.

She was too numb and emotional from being in the wrong place at the wrong time and was now worried for her family's safety. Life for the Stevens family was about to drastically change!

Chapter 7

"We know who she is. Let's go and get her before she spills her guts," Oleg coldly suggested as they drove into the secure compound. Everyone was yelling at each other, agitated at their lapse of judgment regarding that night's business dealings. The pharmaceutical rep was supposed to have helped broker a mega-million-dollar deal for the Kozlovs, and now the whole thing had been derailed in a moment of uncontrolled anger at a flippant response from Carson. The money was gone, and a witness was on the loose who could ID all three of them — it was a wonder they didn't shoot each other over it all! The men were hot and bothered and eventually downed a bottle of their favorite Russian liquor to help calm their nerves.

Oleg had followed the Kozlovs to the U.S. and was their designated 'taskmaster' on all things egregious! He was single and had a checkered past in Russia, mostly because of his black-market activities. Oleg was ruthless and ugly, with many a battle scar on his neck and arms but committed to the Kozlovs for his survival and that of their businesses. He was the first to remind the brothers of Sarah's identity and quickly proposed the solution to get rid of her that night.

"It's too late!" Pavel exclaimed as he hung up the phone. "She's already at the police station, singing like a bird. It's only a matter of time before we have visitors. We need to line up our alibi and call our lawyers. Tell me—who's on call tonight to deliver a message to this woman? I want her to know there are consequences to her actions… And I want this to happen *now!*"

Oleg knew whom to call for the perfect message to be delivered to Sarah and her family. This powerful crime family had paid associates everywhere — which included two wayward officers in need of some financial help at the local police station. One of them had just confirmed that Sarah and her husband were reviewing incriminating photos at the station.

"Perfect," Pavel said, somewhat satisfied, and instructed Oleg to make his call.

Chapter 8

Nicholas jumped into the first squad car to be sent out to get Susan, who was at home with Max. He had requested that both his daughter and dog be picked up together. He had called Susan first to get her packing so he would have some time to do a small bit for himself and get some items together for Max. Nicholas had the hardest job and knew he would need the most time to get it all done under the watchful/protective eyes of his escorts. Susan would have too many questions to address and had to just trust her dad and pack.

Meanwhile, Sarah tried to regain some of her composure to call Sophie and Jackson to briefly explain the immediate need to join the family. She instructed each of them to bring any items needed as if going away for a couple of weeks but would be caught short without those items if they didn't hustle. Each of the kids realized something serious had happened to their mom — they could hear it in her voice and trusted her word on preparing and not sharing with anyone else. Sarah was always direct and quick on her feet, which helped with her patients and now served her well with her own family in flight. The second squad car was dispatched to retrieve Jackson from his apartment. Sophie and her husband, Austin, were to be collected by a third patrol.

By the time they had all assembled at the police station, it was after two a.m.

They all were tired and confused as they entered the holding room where their mother was being kept.

"Oh my God… mom!!" The kids each cried out at seeing their mom worn out, face blotchy from crying, and wearing blood-stained clothes. They rushed to her.

"Mom… what happened… are you OK?" Susan started to tear up and she was the first to step in and hug her mom with the others tightening up the group hug behind her. Tears were shed and questions fired out. And through it all, Max, the faithful family dog, initially happy to see his whole family together, sat silently on guard next to Sarah as if he knew something wasn't right with her. He must have wondered why the family was gathered in this strange place and sensed the confusion at the late hour.

Sarah needed to get their things as well, but not until the family was safe at the station. With a small army of police and FBI officers, Nicholas returned to their home to help Sarah pack on the fly and for him to close up the house and make sure it would be okay while they were gone. But before exiting the official FBI-issued van with tinted windows, a protective squadron of officers scoured the home and surrounding area to make sure it was safe to allow the exhausted couple to enter. There was a time limit on how long they had before the mandatory exit would be called - Sarah walked into her closet and just stared at her clothes before finally grabbing a suitcase from the top shelf to fill it up while officers oversaw the perimeter. Nicholas was across the hall doing the same thing in his office, filling his briefcase with essential work items and unfinished projects that would need his attention. It was a good thing this was all happening while the neighbors were asleep; Sarah didn't want them to know the trouble her family was in!

"TIME!" one of the agents called out which meant time to go regardless of whether Sarah and Nicholas were ready or not.

Working quickly, Sarah managed to delegate the watering of the few indoor plants she had not yet killed to an idle agent, grabbed her Walkman, and snagged her favorite family photo to put up wherever they wound up. As she walked out the door of the two-story Tuscany-style fixer-upper they had bought twenty-five years ago, a wave of nostalgia and sadness hit her. This was where they had raised their kids, made a house into their home, and knew their neighbors as good friends. She loved their home and the memories created there. Another sick feeling overcame her, and she wondered if she had anything left in her stomach to throw up.

Just as the entourage walked out the front door towards the van, a large explosion erupted in the de-tached garage. The blast lit it up in a ball of fire, de-stroying it completely. The force of the explosion knocked the group to the ground and caused them to yell and scramble towards the van. While Sarah was screaming in shocked disbelief at the near miss and destruction of their garage, the agents got the pair up and into the van, yelling "GO GO GO!" to the driver to quickly get out of there before anyone saw them.

Chapter 9

As husband and wife walked into the briefing room to rejoin their family, Sarah broke down and sobbed uncontrollably once again at the sight of seeing her family safe and all together. Another immediate group hug took over to help soothe her nerves. Many people came and went into the room. Words were spoken, but Sarah was exhausted, in shock, and didn't hear them; she just needed to be with her family as they continued to ask questions to whoever was present. Sarah didn't tell her family about the bombing.

The FBI had arranged for the Stevens family to be moved to a more secure and secret location. All electronic devices were collected from them, rules were spewed with warnings about breaking them, and the possible consequences of being found by the Kozlov brothers were laid out in great detail. Each family member had to acknowledge their understanding of the predicament and subsequent consequences if the outlined procedures were not followed. As people moved about to make it all happen, the stress level of those involved increased when they found out that Steven's garage had just been bombed only a few hours after the murder. It was apparent that this whole ordeal was a *big* deal with the number of agents moving about in the middle of the night making arrangements to transport the Stevens family. The FBI was salivating at the chance to finally have a case against the Kozlovs, hoping to put them behind bars forever, but needed to quickly get the family to safety and confirm Sarah's willingness to testify.

It was early morning, and the time had finally arrived to move the family to the secure location. The six family members, Max, and two supporting agents all got into a large, bulletproof, unmarked van. After a bit of a drive, the van pulled up to a large, official-looking brown building and drove down a ramp into what looked like a secure, underground loading area that may have been used in the past for transporting important people or prisoners. From this checkpoint, they were moved into one of the seven unmarked FBI vans under the watchful eyes of the same two agents whom Sarah had met earlier. The staging area was void of any other agents or personnel to keep people from knowing which van the family would ultimately ride in. After they were loaded in and quiet, the drivers of the vans were allowed to get in to start their respective journeys. Each van left at the same time, with the same approximate weight load aboard, but with each driving off in a different direction in case anyone was watching from afar.

After riding for what seemed like an hour or so, the sleepy family was successfully delivered to a 'safe house', which didn't look anything *like* a house. Rather, they were taken to the basement of a sterile-looking facility with numerous gates and doors that required codes and badges to open. As they walked into their 'home', it was apparent that they would be safely buried at the bottom of some building where no one could see or have access to them. The protective compound had no windows. Inside it felt like what Sarah thought a room aboard a spacecraft might look like: sterile and plain. Despite the lack of any style, it seemed like someone had *tried* to add some homey touches. There were throw blankets on the sofas, teddy bears on the beds, children's books - with family favorite *Goodnight Moon* on the coffee table - board games stacked neatly on the shelf, and a lot of G-rated VHS tapes to pick from. Sarah guessed the powers that be thought only happy and nonviolent movies would be appropriate for whoever was living here, and they were right. The last thing this family would need to watch, having missed a garage bombing and seeing a gruesome murder, was a 'Godfather' type movie!

The first order of business was to get everyone settled into their new rooms. Aspirin, water, and snacks were handed out to help calm the nerves and headaches. Everything was organized by a nice, matronly woman who greeted the family as they arrived and asked to be called Mrs. Mueller. She would act as a bridge between the family and the FBI in getting provisions and other items needed during their stay. Mrs. Mueller exuded a caring and trustful demeanor to all she met. With her gray hair pulled back in a bun and wearing a long dress, one would think she was someone's grandmother. But the reality was that Mrs. Mueller was a highly respected and decorated agent who had retired from the field and was currently using her skills to monitor those that had to inhabit the Cal-WRAP (California Witness Relocation and Assistance Program) facility. Mrs. Mueller observed the occupants and provided important information to the agents and attorneys handling the case. She had been called in and had been waiting for the family to arrive.

The four-bedroom 'home' was fully stocked like a five-star hotel and then some. The Stevens were lucky to have had a few precious minutes to pack some clothes, as most previous inhabitants didn't get any time to grab their pets, let alone a toothbrush, due to their dire circumstances and immediate threats. The Stevens attempted to run through their own bedtime routines, but most failed and just hit the pillows hard. Sarah made sure she spent time with them individually to provide comfort, reassurance, and hugs. She even waited for the lights to go out in each room before finally collapsing on her pillow.

Nicholas was already fast asleep. He had found a mini bar of sorts and felt it appropriate to desensitize his nerves and brain the only way he knew how to — with an alcoholic beverage. Poor guy — she couldn't blame him for passing out but had thought maybe he might want to talk first. Yet the shock and speed at which their world was shattered was a lot for them both. Sarah figured a quick shower would help her to relax a bit. When she got out it was early morning. with the sun about to rise outside their windowless prison. Completely exhausted, Sarah tried not to think about what she had been through as she closed her eyes and drifted off. Just then, Max walked into her room and put his nose up against her arm, staring up as if to ask what was going on.

"Oh Max, if you only knew, boy," she said in a soothing voice. "Go lie down, buddy."

And he did, but by the door, providing a barrier to anyone wanting to enter. Faithful Max had just had his world rocked as well, and there wasn't any way of explaining it to him, but somehow Sarah thought he understood. He had been by their sides the whole evening, not once barking or interfering with all the intruders and interrogators. Just knowing Max was there helped calm her down, finally allowing Sarah to fall asleep at last.

Chapter 10

Everyone slept in and needed it. Even Sarah slumbered way past her routine hour and woke with panic racing through her veins as she realized Max hadn't been fed or let out! She quickly got up, sadly realizing that the previous evening's events had not been a nightmare but a harsh reality that needed to be dealt with. She quickly put on the FBI safe house-issued robe and entered the living room to find Mrs. Mueller sitting quietly and petting Max.

"Good morning, Dr. Stevens," she said. "Since I've been assigned to be your temporary house manager, I not only help coordinate your meals, but I also help with your other needs. I've already taken Max out and fed him. We have a secluded yard for pets, and one of our agents stationed at your home told us what kind of dog food he found in one of your cupboards, so that's what we got him. I hope that was alright. We figured you all needed some extra rest."

"Yes. *Yes!*" Sarah wearily smiled, pleasantly surprised by the nice gesture, and forward-thinking of Mrs. Mueller.

"I'm sure the rest of my family will be up soon. How does the breakfast meal thing work around here?"

"You just need to prepare a grocery list of items your family might need or want and submit it to me. Your first grocery list from today can be delivered fairly quickly — but the others will have a 24-hour delay so think ahead," Mrs. Mueller replied. "You'll prepare your own meals and if you open up the cupboards you'll see what we already stocked them with." Secretly, Sarah was hoping an FBI-issued chef would magically appear to prepare her family's meals but no such luck.

This was a heck of a way to have family mealtime, which didn't happen often due to the hectic schedules and different residences of the Stevens family. Turning lemons into lemonade would be the challenge for the day, so Sarah quickly thought out several menus, wrote out what was needed after checking the sparsely stocked cupboards, and hoped it would be delivered before the family awoke.

While Mrs. Mueller was gone, Sarah groggily

got into her a.m. routine, sprucing up using some of her own toiletries to hide the dark circles under her eyes, all without waking up Nicholas. By the time Mrs. Mueller returned with the groceries; Sarah was ready to prepare a big brunch that included something everyone liked. The table was just set when Nicholas walked into the room with a surprised look upon seeing his wife in the kitchen attempting to prepare a meal.

"Wow! Just when I'd thought I'd seen it all, another surprise — you in the kitchen!" he teased. "I don't think I can take any more surprises. Time to talk?"

"Nah, let's get everyone up, showered, dressed, et cetera, then we'll sit down and do it as a family. We all have questions and concerns, so let's do it together to avoid repeating ourselves."

Nodding in agreement, Nicholas planted an extra-long kiss on his wife's lips and gave her a long reassuring hug. After going through a couple of cupboards, he grabbed a cup of joe and proceeded to see if he could conquer the TV remote to see what was happening in the real world.

After eleven a.m., Sarah knocked on

everyone's doors. Due to the previous night's jarring events, they all uncharacteristically got up quickly and moved to get ready for something they didn't know anything about. Taking Sarah's cue, Max made his rounds as well, acting as the compound ambassador, giving everyone a doggie goober kiss here and there. Max was the only real and welcome routine in this new environment.

The family slowly walked around the small 'home' checking out the essentials and making small talk. They were relieved to see their parents in the kitchen.

"I'm sure you all have a lot of questions and we will answer them. Let's get some breakfast going and then we'll talk... how about it?" Sarah asked, hoping for simple compliance.

Gathered at the kitchen table to eat, Sarah wasn't sure if her family had noticed her orchestration of the meal. But all were jolted by the door opening and three FBI agents filing in, looking official with their clipboards and briefcases. Mrs. Mueller took her cue to leave them all to do their work. The men's presence was enough for the forks to be put down and discussions stopped. The Stevens family didn't know what was coming at them or what their lives were going to be like afterward.

Chapter 11

FBI Director Nathan Vargas was the oldest son of immigrant Spaniards and properly introduced himself and the other agents.

"Good morning – please keep eating - and while you are doing that, I'm going to start explaining what we have here, and what will happen to get your case finished ASAP."

Even though he encouraged everyone to continue with their meal it was too late. Director Vargas had a presence about him that they felt when he first started to talk, and no one wanted indigestion. He had clearly seen a lot and commanded great respect from his underlings. His experience was vast, diplomacy tops, and agency awards too numerous to count. He intimidated all who worked with and for him — and though his Brooklyn accent had faded, his street smarts had not... Today, he met with one of the most important and difficult assignments of his career.

Director Vargas started into his assessment of the situation, going into detail about what Sarah had witnessed and the severity of the situation the family was now in because of it. Susan immediately went over to sit next to her mom while listening to the bad news. Yet there was good news to share, too.

"We arrested the two Kozlov brothers two hours ago," Vargas said. "Both are being detained without bail due to the severity of the crimes they were accused of and who they are. Legal proceedings will start soon."

While the rest of the family cheered, Sarah didn't. "Why wasn't the third one arrested? There was a third one!" she declared. She feared the ordeal was far from over.

Director Vargas took a deep breath and looked at his colleagues as if to get the courage needed to say what needed to be said in front of the family. "The whereabouts of Oleg Sokotov are unknown at this time. He was probably the one behind the bombing of your garage."

"WHAT??... did our house burn down too... is it all gone Mom... Dad?" Jackson blurted out with tears welling up in his eyes at the thought of their childhood home being gone. The other family members were also shocked to hear about the garage and started to zing questions back and forth for answers.

"Mr. Vargas... what happened to our home?" Jackson asked again.

"Nothing happened to your house. Your home is still intact," Director Vargas assured them. "Just the garage was damaged. Three agents have been assigned to watch your home and have set up cameras and motion detectors in case Oleg Sokotov or another thug decides to pay a visit."

One of the agents asked to speak separately with Nicholas to get a list of all vendors who might visit or service their home over the next forty-five days. Fortunately, it was Saturday, so no one in the Stevens family would be missing work or school. Instead, they now had time to figure out their excuses for being away and would get some help from the agents to concoct and implement their stories.

"Can the agents staying in our home say that they're relatives or friends house sitting?" asked Nicholas. "They can say they're helping with the clean-up due to a water-tank explosion, so we can continue to enjoy our vacation away?"

Before the director could respond, Susan blurted out, "What about Claire? We have to call Claire and make sure she's safe!" Susan yelled.

Their amazing housekeeper had always managed to sneak in special holiday treats and other assorted goodies to Susan while her parents were at work. Susan wanted to make sure Claire was taken care of.

"Don't worry," Nicholas assured his daughter "We'll give Claire a month-long paid vacation. I'm sure she will appreciate it."

The last thing Claire needed was to show up and see the garage blown to pieces and walk in the house catching the various agents off guard or have them pulling their guns out at her! The vacation story seemed plausible, so it was agreed upon and sent up and down the communication lines to implement as the cover story. Nicholas made a note to call Claire, or to at least find out how to make the call from their secure location.

Another agent laid out a whole list of what the

family could and couldn't do while living in the compound. They would need permission for just about everything they did that wasn't personal in nature. Failure to abide by the rules would come with a heavy price. They all acknowledged the seriousness and signed forms agreeing to the terms and conditions of their new lifestyle. Each received a copy to review, while another copy was taped to the refrigerator as a constant reminder — as if anyone could forget!

"So how long are we going to be here? I have class on Monday, mom, and dad… don't you have to be at work?" Jackson was concerned for everyone, and they all stared at the Director for answers. However, the question of how long they would be held captive in the compound couldn't be answered. No one knew when Sarah would be testifying.

Director Vargas went into detail about the legalities and formalities of the case against the Kozlov brothers and how the FBI had unsuccessfully tried to infiltrate their crime ring for years.

"Dr. Stevens, you happened to witness a murder that could put the Kozlovs away forever," the director stated with a supportive smile as other agents chimed in with their support and protocols towards the process.

Sarah thought the agents assumed too much — that she would testify against the Kozlovs thereby ending their mission to see them found guilty. Not once did they ask how she felt about her involvement or if she would even testify. It appeared that the agents used an assumptive approach with Sarah which didn't sit well with her or the family. Sarah thought if there had been a bottle of Champagne nearby, the agents probably would have opened it to prematurely celebrate their expected victory!

Sarah was fully awake and feeling the effects of her caffeinated morning drink kicking in and her analytical mind churning away.

"I need to speak to my lawyer about all this!" she blurted out.

The room went silent as she added, "There's a lot going on here, and I need to have an unbiased opinion about what my family and I, should or shouldn't be doing. The last fifteen hours have been a whirlwind and I need to get some legal guidance given the severity of this whole situation."

The stunned agents quickly realized that Sarah's shock had worn off; her clear thinking was both rational and warranted, given the precarious situation. The fact was, she didn't have a lawyer for something like this; she would need to call her financial planning advisor and hope that the advisor had a referral who wasn't connected in some way to the Kozlov family. The odds were low that this would be a problem; Sarah just knew she needed another clear head to help represent her in something she was clueless about. After a few comments between themselves, Director Vargas agreed that she could hire her own attorney to work with the government's attorneys on the case but with more conditions tied to it on the logistics on how they could safely meet outside the compound.

Then the three agents left the family to silently pick at what was left on their plates. But who could eat at a time like this? The ordeal was all they could talk about. The family had more questions than what little answers existed and wanted to know all the details. Sarah did her best to answer what she could.

After the dishes were done, Sarah and Nicholas talked privately about how they might navigate the days ahead and what they should share with their family as new details emerged related to the case. They weren't sure if full disclosure was needed or how the active family would handle life in the confined compound. For now, they felt safe, but for how long? After a quick, supportive hand-holding conversation on the couch and a mental review of what she heard the agents say, Sarah suggested that she go alone to meet the attorney while Nicholas stayed with the family. After a bit of quibbling, he agreed to stay behind, though he felt she needed him more than their grown kids did. Sarah followed the dialing rules on the safe-house phone and called her financial planner for assistance and a referral.

Chapter 12

"Hey, Jackie! You're never going to guess what the purpose of this call is about! Can you talk now? I need some serious help with a referral."

Sarah went into guarded detail with her faithful financial planner, who had not only guided her family's financial affairs for twenty-plus years but had also taken the time to teach her about the financial world and how to make great, long-term decisions. Her financial planner had become a trusted friend who immediately referred her to Anthony Benowitz, a former prosecutor and now a successful private defense attorney that had a reputation as one of the best legal minds in town. After being cleared by the FBI, Sarah felt safe in seeking his legal guidance and confiding all the assorted details of her dilemma to him. Sarah called Anthony, who after a lengthy conversation agreed to take her case.

To keep the family's whereabouts unknown,

Anthony was instructed to drive to a pre-assigned location before being transported to the safe house in the back of a blackout security van to meet with Sarah, Director Vargas, and the agents on the case. While being driven to the unusual meeting spot, he was reminded of the confidentiality of the case and ramifications by both the FBI and Kozlovs should he violate it or in any way jeopardized the safety of the Stevens family or the pending court case. Anthony was known as a tough negotiator; FBI Director Vargas was not looking forward to working with him.

Anthony walked into a secluded room full of listening devices and cameras, introduced himself to all around the table, and saw Sarah for the first time, standing to introduce herself. After thirty-five years of practicing law, the experienced attorney was nearing retirement due to health problems that had left him bald, wearing thick glasses, and experiencing sporadic back pain. Despite all that, he was drawn to the case, although he found his stature somewhat dwarfed by Director Vargas' authoritative demeanor and size. Anthony had worked hard to achieve his partner status at the firm that now included his name in its moniker, but nothing had prepared him for what he would be dealing with in Sarah's case.

Director Vargas led the discussion and briefed Anthony on the details and complexities involved. Anthony had heard about the Kozlovs but had never worked on any cases that involved them nor met them. Sarah listened intently and tried hard to understand what the desired game plan was as it formed during the briefing.

After hours of long and emotional discussions, Sarah asked, and then demanded the impossible and, after much argument, got it: a one-on-one conversation with her attorney alone, away from the compound, in an isolated area that didn't have any listening devices or cameras. The blackout van delivered the two of them to a large, public park where they sat down on a swing set for fear that the recommended park table might be bugged or too close to the van. Sarah knew the FBI would keep close tabs on her and would not want one of their most valuable assets to disappear or get hurt.

Chapter 13

After observing his client for signs of stress, Anthony cautiously asked, "How are you feeling, Dr. Stevens? I can only imagine what you're going through with the pressure of your family's lives hanging in the balance. You were pretty quiet during most of the discussion with Director Vargas."

Sarah sucked back her emotions and swallowed hard for fear of letting the dam break. She looked Anthony squarely in the eye and asked, "I need you to be honest - am I screwed? Is there any way out of this that doesn't include me or my family getting killed? I've thought a lot about this and can't seem to find a safe way out given the third guy is still on the loose and the type of violence these people are involved with."

She kept her gaze unwaveringly on her lawyer. Would there be any sign of hope - or would he hesitate, while trying to figure out how to deliver bad news? Sarah was extremely good at reading people. It was part of her job to get information from her young patients and their parents to recommend the best course of medical treatment. She was superb at negotiating, and her people-reading skills came in handy whenever she played a friendly game of poker with her extended family during the holidays. Anthony squirmed a bit and hesitated — Sarah's heart skipped a beat. She already knew about her limited options — options that were inadequate because, over the long run, they wouldn't ensure the survival of her family. Her floodgate wanted to break releasing her stress and emotions. She needed to focus.

Anthony began his assessment. "If your testimony stands, and the Kozlov brothers are sent to prison, it's likely that they will still attempt to get to you, as long as Oleg Sokotov is at large. And even if they catch him," the attorney grimly continued, "the Kozlovs have other associates who can execute a contract on your life. And if this court case fails and the Kozlovs are released on some technicality, things won't look good for you. To be completely frank, I'm worried you are doomed — either way!"

No matter how Sarah thought about her options, the outcomes were all bad. All she could think about was her family being hurt by these monsters. She put her head in her hands and started to sob.

And then it hit her.

She looked up as if startled. It was a crazy idea that popped into her head, but for now, it was her only safe way out. She asked Anthony for a notepad and a pen, which he quickly retrieved from his briefcase.

Sarah carefully explained her idea as if arguing with herself as she filled in the blanks. Anthony and Sarah sat together for three hours, making a list of what was needed to be said or done while hammering out as many details as possible. They went back and forth asking each other questions about possibilities and circumstances. Anthony wrote as fast as he could to capture the details and essence of her brilliant idea. It was obviously apparent that she would eventually need his help and support in communicating the details of this new plan to the FBI.

"What are these?" Asked Anthony, pointing to some of the items being developed on her plan.

Sarah explained some items further — then followed up to confirm with Anthony, "Do you think this is a hard yes or no?" Anthony was impressed at the coolness with which she handled the questions and planning. She had concocted what seemed to be a way out while under enormous pressure, and if everyone played their part correctly, it could work. They had a good rough draft and would need to meet again to work out the finer points. Until then, they agreed that neither of them would talk about it with anyone else.

The setting sun reminded Sarah of the need to go 'home' and see her family. Sarah knew the trial was being expedited which meant her plan would need to be agreed upon and then implemented.... SOON. Sarah knew she needed to fill in more blanks - and may have missed a few important points- but she had something more than she did before.

She had hope.

Chapter 14

Sarah walked in the door of the safehouse, where all three of her adult children ran up to hug her, much like they did years ago when they were little kids when she arrived home from a full workday. How sweet it was back then to have them yelling and excited to see her.

She held onto them for a few precious seconds longer than normal to absorb their love and concern before asking them about their day in their makeshift home.

Nicholas joined in on the questions and chatter, noticing his wife's changed demeanor; she seemed a bit more at ease this evening. His wife was the glue and foundation of their family. If she smiled and was happy, it trickled over into everyone's life.

Later that night, while she tried to sleep, Sarah's mind raced as she played out the details of her plan, trying to think of all the possible scenarios, both positive and negative. Eventually, she tiptoed out of the bedroom to find some paper and a pen. She was up for three more hours jotting down all her ideas before she crept back into bed. She kept her notes hidden under the mattress, and just knowing they were there made her feel more empowered. Her prayers were being answered and this new-found peace allowed her to finally fall into a well-needed deep sleep.

Chapter 15

Anthony Benowitz had dropped everything to take Sarah's case. He was ready when the FBI called to arrange for him to meet his client in a different park the following morning for security reasons. The FBI kept them under surveillance the entire time and issued a time limit for their meeting. Although the FBI escort asked them to sit on the picnic tables on the west side of the park, Anthony and Sarah sat on the tables facing north, with their backs to the van to prevent anyone from reading their lips or interpreting their conversations. They left nothing to chance.

Both needed to work quickly to hammer the final details and ideas that Sarah and Anthony had thought about the night before.

"Sarah, I'm not sure if the FBI will allow you to travel outside of the U.S. given the lack of protection available outside our borders so maybe we should work more on the financial remuneration part? And how did you come up with the monthly pension amounts? I'm impressed with your financial knowledge and ideas!"

After hours of back and forth what-if scenarios, and a few loud sneezes from Sarah's exposure to some pollen at the park, Anthony and Sarah developed an agreement that was almost ready to be presented to Director Vargas. Anthony agreed to type up the formal proposal on an offline word processor with no help from any staff for security reasons. His law firm didn't even know of his involvement with the case, but he did build it into the agreement that his legal fees were to be paid by the FBI.

Three copies of the final, confidential agreement would ultimately be generated and signed by both the FBI and Dr. Stevens. One copy would be retained by Anthony in a secure location, one by the FBI, and one by Sarah, with her copy to be placed in a safe deposit box of her choosing. It was a special type of document that would need to be ready in two days. Anthony knew that the FBI's higher-ups would have to evaluate Sarah's proposal and the conditions for her involvement in the Kozlov case, so he spent a considerable amount of time constructing the proposal —

with very little sleep. He also reminded Sarah to have a discussion with Nicholas about the upcoming meeting with the FBI. She needed to explain to her husband that only she could attend this meeting, by orders of the agency. Sarah also needed to keep the contents of her deal a secret from her family for their protection; she would need a good poker face to pull it all off.

The FBI wanted nothing more than to succeed with the convictions. The agency could taste the success, but they would have to pay a price to support their star witness.

Chapter 16

Sarah returned to the FBI compound in the bulletproof, blacked-out van. She now had *hope,* and Anthony was moving in the right direction in constructing 'the agreement'.

Her family was happy to see her walk in and once again the kids formed a circle of hugs around their mom, which she needed and appreciated. After the greeting, Sarah noticed how the kids were acting more normal with their familiar nitpicking at each other and some arguing over who Max would be sleeping with. It was apparent that they were experiencing cabin fever and needed to get out for some sort of activity. Anything that was out of the compound and away from the reminders of the danger they were in was needed. Sarah asked the always-friendly Mrs. Mueller to relay a family field trip request up the ladder, but within minutes of her call, the request was denied citing security issues. Sarah quickly asked for Director Vargas' phone number to get the answer she was looking for.

"Mr. Vargas, we need a break from this compound. We are grateful to have it, but if we are to survive this ordeal, we need to see the blue sky once again. May I offer an original idea?"

"I'm sitting down Dr. Stevens, what is your idea?" he said.

Sarah went into detail about how the Stevens family could be outside for a day without anyone being the wiser for it. After a heated debate with him about his concerns, she got what she wanted to hear — a *yes*! The FBI director was walking a fine line keeping his star witness safe, happy, and willing to testify. Director Vargas was preparing for the meeting with both Sarah and her attorney in two days, so he approved the outing with a few conditions, one of which was to always have disguised agents with them. Sarah happily agreed and thanked the director for his flexibility.

Running into the family room where all were gathered, Sarah yelled, "I just witnessed a gruesome crime and am confined with my favorite family. So, guess where are we going?" Her family looked at her like she had just snapped and lost her mind! Nicholas caught on that something good was about to happen and played along to break the awkward silence. "I have a guess?" he smiled and Sarah shouted, "we're going to Disneyland… in disguise!" Everyone, including Mrs. Mueller, laughed and cheered for the first time since entering the compound.

When the kids were younger, Nicholas and Sarah took them to Disneyland every year and always had a fabulous time playing together as a family. How could they not when visiting 'the happiest place on earth?' Sarah had bargained to allow her family this outing, and they were elated. Everyone was wondering what their disguises were going to be and already started to plan what rides they would conquer first. It was the best evening in the dreary compound so far…. laced with the hope for a great day together sans anything having to do with the upcoming trial. Hope was spreading.

Chapter 17

The next morning, as the family ate breakfast together, a knock at the door revealed Mrs. Mueller, who had brought them boxes filled with professional makeup, wigs, and clothes that included written instructions on how to use them all!

Sophie had attended drama classes while in school and took the lead, helping everyone get into their disguises, which included a brief makeup lesson. The wigs changed the girls' hair color and length, with their long hair now under a skull cap. Jackson and Austin were each given a mustache and Nicholas an older white beard and fake belly, which all agreed made him look fifteen years older and a possible relative of Santa. Sarah opted for a more mature look as well, sporting a cane, gray wig, and older-looking dress to play the family matriarch. There were lots of giggles and laughter while they practiced getting ready and perfecting their looks. Even Max was included in the plan and given a 'therapy dog in training' vest to wear!

Oh, how they wanted a photo to remember their looks, but that would have been against the rules. Besides, they didn't have any way to take a picture, since all their cameras and electronics had been collected before their first entrance into the safe house, except for Sarah's Walkman since it wasn't connected to the internet. Nicholas turned the stereo on for all to hear some music while they practiced and prepared for a fun day.

It didn't matter that cameras weren't allowed. The Stevens would be headed out, dressed up, 'goofy' looking, and most importantly, together. They wouldn't be reminded of their ordeal, only whimsical fun and games would occupy their time and thoughts for the day - even though four agents would be accompanying them - with four more watching from afar. Director Vargas had said to be ready to go at 7:00 the next morning, but all were up, fed, disguised, and eagerly ready by 6:45!

During the long drive to Disneyland, the rules and protocols for the day were discussed, along with the consequences if broken. All happily agreed to the regulations and just wanted to get out of the van and into the theme park. Keeping tabs on a family of six plus Max would not be easy. Given the crowded park atmosphere, the agents took turns accompanying them in the lines and even joining them on the rides. It was an FBI-escort nightmare, but Director Vargas had been convinced that the odds of anyone looking for them in disguise at Disneyland were just too remote.

Sarah's mind was split trying to enjoy the day while remembering all the times she and Nicholas had taken the kids there and the carefree fun they had enjoyed together. They would make a weekend of it, trying to hit as many attractions and rides as they could before a child had a meltdown or needed a nap. As they got older, the kids started to outlast their parents, who watched from afar as they hit every centrifugal force ride the park had to offer. Nicholas and Sarah would catch up on 'life' while the kids did their thing. But today, even the older-looking matriarch surprised onlookers by going on *all* the rides. Sarah didn't want to miss a moment laughing with her family and experiencing the energy of the park. Gone were any hesitations of who would ride with whom; they all took turns, even if it meant an agent might be sitting with them. Max loved the attention from his family, various park visitors, and the agent assigned to wait with him while the family took the rides. The agents couldn't help but have a good time, too, laughing along with the family they were there to protect!

The field trip was deemed a success, and all hoped that further outings might be allowed during their brief stay. When they arrived back at the secure compound, it was obvious everyone was tired but happy for the break. Being together and blowing off some steam worked for the whole family, including the attention stealer Max, who bunked with Jackson for the night.

Chapter 18

A familiar agent knocked on the compound door at 9:00 a.m. to remind Sarah that she had a meeting with the FBI attorneys to strategize for the trial, now scheduled to start in three weeks. She stepped out and closed the door behind her to shield her family from her remarks.

"Has Director Vargas spoken to my lawyer?" she asked. "Anthony said I can't meet with your attorneys until he does."

Anthony had discussed portions of the agreement with the FBI director while the Stevens family was at Disneyland. Sarah knew she had the best bargaining chip in getting what she wanted and stood her ground.

"Please have Director Vargas come talk to me if he has any questions," she gently added and made it known that she was done with the conversation. As the agent left Sarah breathed a sigh of relief knowing someone would eventually be back to discuss her proposal. When that time came, she would request her attorney be present as well. Sarah was about to make the deal of her life and would need all the help she could get if her plan was to succeed!

The same agent returned the next morning, only this time he was prepared to inform Sarah that she and her attorney needed to be ready to go by 1:00 p.m. for a ride to the director's temporary office, to discuss her request. She called Anthony, who after asking a few more questions about the deal, confirmed he was ready to go. His life had been placed on hold to handle this case, which had made his calendar flexible for upcoming meetings and unforeseen discussions about Sarah's deal, even if it cost him some sleep.

Sarah's security detail and three-van entourage picked up Anthony later that morning. As he entered the bulletproof van and took his seat next to Sarah, he noticed the accompanying agents were all wearing bulletproof vests and that the privacy panel was up to keep the agents in the front seat from seeing or hearing what was happening in the back. They patted him down quickly before giving him the green light to proceed. It was a bit intimidating just to ride in the van, let alone to see the other vans on each side and agents wearing the protective vests.

Sarah was nervous but vowed not to be intimidated by her circumstances or the director's office. She had played out the possible conversations and scenes over and over in her mind the night before, trying to get a handle on how she should act and react while Nicholas, unaware of his wife's pending test, slept comfortably next to her. She was used to being in an authoritative role with her patients and their families, but this was an entirely different situation.

Little was said during the ride to the director's office, but Anthony did hand his client a file with the agreement in it and asked her to quietly review it while in transit. Sarah did this quickly, not knowing how long the car ride would take through the horrible traffic. As she finished, she gave Anthony a nod of approval and said she was ready for the discussion, which would be more like a negotiation. He shared a few last-minute suggestions that would allow him to represent her in the best light as they pulled up to the cold-looking building that housed the local FBI field operations.

Chapter 19

Driving into the secure, underground parking area was a trip all by itself, given the multiple times their driver had to submit to badge and vehicle checks. The underbelly of the van was inspected, with more badges checked and forms shared. As the three vans pulled up to their final checkpoint and were cleared, all the occupants got out. The agents immediately formed a protective circle around Sarah, with Anthony walking behind the group into the building and through even more checkpoints within. It was obvious to Sarah and her attorney that they were in a very secure building.

The entourage was guided to a large, windowless conference room that had the latest security technology available for its time. They took their seats and were offered something to drink.

Director Vargas entered the room, dismissed all but two of the agents, and tossed a file onto the table in front of him as he sat down.

The director asked how the family was doing, if they were comfortable in the safehouse, and how they enjoyed Disneyland. After this bit of small talk, he got down to business, thanking Sarah once again for reporting what she saw and for being a participant in justice being served. She thought the director was laying it on a bit thick but listened carefully and watched for clues as to what her future would be like. He was tough to read.

"No one in the history of the FBI has ever been given such a deal as the one Mr. Benowitz sent me this morning," Director Vargas began. "Usually it's the criminals who beg for mercy and try to create a plea bargain for their lives to be spared in some way. But *never* a witness—not like this!" All eyes in the room were upon him as he continued.

"Given the extent of Dr. Stevens' demands and the impending court date, I want to urge her to move forward and start preparations for the trial," he said. "The weeks ahead will be trying enough. I recommend that Dr. Stevens leave the details of her 'deal' on the table for a later, less stressful time to finish."

Just as Anthony was about to speak, Sarah

stood up to take command of the conversation. "I'd like to remind Director Vargas and the FBI of the sacrifice, risks, and stress my family would be under if I testify," she stated emphatically. "We would pay the ultimate price for any mistakes by the agency. There is no way my family can be promised safety or protected forever. If the trial doesn't go as planned, and the Kozlov brothers get a light sentence—or worse yet, if the case gets thrown out of court and they all walk—it would spell disaster for all of us! And you still don't even know where the third culprit is."

In her eyes, there was no way out, other than through her proposal.

"I am not about to roll the dice!" she declared. "I want to control my fate so let's get this agreement done now while we're all together."

Anthony chimed in, suggesting that it was time to go through the details of Sarah's plan, a plan that would forever be known as 'The Sacrificial Deal.'

The director excused the other agents, giving them instructions that all recording and listening devices be turned off as they left the room.

Chapter 20

The Sacrificial Deal, as penned by Dr. Sarah
Stevens before her lawyer added the legal terminology.

1) The Stevens family will have round-the-clock
   protection at their home for at least one year,
   or however long they want, unless FBI intelligence or circumstances show otherwise
   needed. Nicholas Stevens will make the final
   decision regarding when to terminate the protection.

2) The FBI will assign one, and only one, agent to
   know of Dr. Stevens' whereabouts and will be
   her assigned contact for the duration of this
   contract.

3) The assigned agent will help Dr. Stevens fake
   her own death and then put her into the Witness Protection Program under his sole direction, guidance, and placement.

4) A death certificate will be issued for Dr. Sarah Stevens for Mr. Nicholas Stevens to use in settling her affairs and collecting her life insurance proceeds.

5) The FBI or other agency will deposit $750,000 into Dr. Stevens' new bank account within three days of item #3 and will allow her to manage it as she sees fit. The FBI or any others will not have any claim to it after the deposit is made.

6) The Stevens family can receive counseling for as long as they want with a family therapist of their choosing. Price will not be an issue nor negotiated with the therapist via agency demands or limits. The family (either as a whole or individually) can receive the counseling until Mr. Stevens directs otherwise.

7) The FBI or other agency will pay Dr. Stevens a monthly pension of $18,000 tax-free. It is to be paid for the rest of her life, whether or not she is in the Witness Protection Program. Payments will begin within three days of item #3.

8) Dr. Stevens will be allowed to secretly see her family while in disguise and without their knowledge once every six months (approximately) or twice a year, with the assigned agent's help. She will have access to use the Agency's plane (and at the Agency's expense) to return to Santa Barbara or wherever her family is for the secret observations.

9) Dr. Stevens will take professional make-up, hair, and costume lessons via private instruction before her court date to prepare for item #8.

10) The agent assigned to Dr. Stevens will do reconnaissance work on the Stevens family to determine which events/observations Dr. Stevens can safely attend without compromising her identity and will propose the visits to her. Director Vargas will use agency intelligence to help provide the assigned agent information on the Stevens family for the timing of the visits.

11) If the Kozlov brothers are convicted and Oleg Sokotov found and incarcerated and/or the

three of them die, Dr. Stevens will be free to
leave the Witness Protection Program and be
reunited with her family at a time and place of
her choosing. Consideration of the remaining
Kozlov crime members and their roles will
also be a determining factor as to whether it is
safe for Dr. Stevens to leave Witness Protection.

12) If Dr. Stevens leaves the Witness Protection
Program and is discovered by an insurance
company, which then files a claim to have the
insurance proceeds from her death reimbursed,
the Agency agrees to fully reimburse the insurance company on behalf of Dr. Stevens and the
family.

13) Dr. Stevens' new assigned home will not be in
severe-weather areas like the desert or in Alaska.
She also has the right to approve the new name
she will be assigned.

14) Dr. Stevens will be able to join Doctors without
Borders to volunteer her time to charity work
outside the U.S. The Agency will help in

establishing her ID to help prove her medical doctor status, to be used only outside of the U.S. and not within.

15) Dr. Stevens is to be given the opportunity to visit her home in the middle of the night before her court date—or when deemed safe by the Agency—to pick up a few items and to put a few needed items in order before the trial. She is to retain her Walkman, one pair of favorite earrings, and one current family photo to be given to her assigned agent to share with her during the secret observations of her family, but not kept by her.

16) The Agency is to procure a DVD bible study series on angels for her to watch with her family before the trial date. Since the Stevens family can't go to church while staying at the compound, this series will help bring that element to them.

17) Three copies of this agreement/deal are to be made and signed. One is to be kept by Dr. Stevens in a safe deposit box at the bank of her choosing using her new assigned identity. One

with Anthony Benowitz who will keep his copy secure and private, and one with FBI Director Nathan Vargas who will confirm that the other copies are secure. Dr. Stevens is to report to Mr. Benowitz that the items listed and agreed to are in motion and/or being done before her trial date, and two times within the next year to again confirm that the agreed-upon arrangements are done or are being done.

Chapter 21

Anthony took the lead and went over every point of the deal in detail, explaining why it was there and how to execute each request. He and Sarah discussed and clarified the details and agreed to adjust a couple of the points Director Vargas suggested, but they were minor in nature.

Director Vargas got Sarah's overall message loud and clear and, in the end, decided to counter by denying two of the seventeen requests to lessen the financial impact to the government. Sarah countered with an even higher allowance to offset the impact that his denial would have on her plan. More than a few words of disbelief were uttered by both sides.

"This is now an all-or-nothing deal," stated Sarah firmly. "Let's flip this around and put you in my shoes. Imagine what *you* would do if YOUR family was at risk of being murdered?"

Director Vargas took a deep breath. He

admired her tenacity and willingness to sacrifice for her family. Sarah had guts and a plan that would ensure her family's ability to continue living their lives with the protection they needed to feel safe. It was brilliant on so many levels that the director found it hard to argue with her and finally gave in. He wanted a conviction, she wanted peace and a way out for her family.

"I'll agree to all of the requests of your deal except for item number fourteen," he said. "The agency can't protect you if you leave the country. Number fourteen is a hard no."

Sarah could live without traveling outside the U.S. and was relieved to hear her deal could then be approved. Both sides agreed to keep the details a secret from everyone given the stakes were so high. For the plan to work, both the FBI and Sarah's family had to be in the dark about what was going to happen. She was adept at being discreet and keeping privileged information on behalf of her patients, but this deal would be the ultimate test of her resolve and willingness to trust her instincts. Her shallow breathing subsided as she felt major progress was beginning to happen. A way out of the nightmare was at hand, and her status as a victim was slightly changing... just a bit.

Sarah really wished she had taken an acting class or two herself, as she would need to hide her emotions during the countdown to the implementation of the plan. Every day would be precious leading up to her court date. But that would be nothing compared to what would follow — navigating a series of emotional rapids with a guide she had never met but would need to entrust her life to — as well as the lives of her family. It was the ultimate leap of faith, but she felt at peace with her decision. As Anthony and Sarah left the conference room, the down-to-business attorney stopped and leaned over to quickly whisper the code word he would use to confirm completion of the agreed-upon arrangements with the FBI. Sarah smiled and knew she would never forget it.

Anthony also wanted to show support and congratulate her on the groundbreaking solution that she had thought up on the fly. Anthony didn't know if he would ever see her again — so he gave her a reassuring hug and a 'don't worry, you will be ok,' look. Although his time with this unique client had been short, he was impressed with her composure and creativeness and sorry he wouldn't be able to see the whole situation play out to its hopeful conclusion. Once the deal was signed, her family would be safe. His job now was to make sure both Sarah and Director Vargas signed the three copies of the agreement. Anthony would keep his copy of The Sacrificial Deal safely stored away and later would confirm she received her copy. He would also ensure that the other elements of the deal were being implemented as agreed upon by using his code word to confirm when they next spoke.

Anthony took in a deep breath and said, "Dr. Stevens, I truly hope this all works out for you and that we may meet again, under better circumstances, to celebrate your victory. You are an amazing woman — one I'll never forget. Best of luck to you!"

And just like that, the two parted ways, left to see how the proverbial chips would fall.

For his part, Director Vargas thought long and hard about which agent to assign to this unique case. He concluded that the experienced Agent Jason would be a perfect match and called him in for his briefing. Agent Jason would only have twenty days to prepare and execute his *own* plan for Dr. Stevens' safety. He would need to move fast. Rumor had it that a large contract had already been issued on her life, information he decided not to share with Sarah.

As Sarah returned to her temporary home, she felt the clock ticking inside her head and heart. She headed for the refrigerator to pour herself a glass of wine leftover from last night's dinner. Max greeted her at the door and received some lavish attention known as the 'Max Rubdown,' where he was quickly rubbed up and down his back. The dog sensed the tension his people were feeling these last few days and had been making his rounds to see them, much like he did at the hospital with Sarah. But tonight, he stuck with her, resting at her feet while the family gathered to watch a movie.

While channel surfing, Nicholas stopped and chuckled, thinking everyone would enjoy the humor of seeing the 1938 version of *The Gangs of New York* playing on cable - but they all booed, hissed, and tossed their freshly popped popcorn at him. Even Sarah nervously laughed and suggested *The Great Race*, a cornball comedy from 1965. It had a happy ending.

Chapter 22

With just days to go before the hearing's started, Sarah reviewed the notes the FBI attorneys prepared for her questioning. They even provided her with a blue suit and scarf to wear in court.

The Sacrificial Deal copies were signed, sealed, and delivered to where they needed to be; she felt the clock moving ever faster as she sped toward her fate. Anthony was paid for his time and was still the only person, outside of the FBI director, who knew of her pending fate but not her future whereabouts. Sarah's next step would be to call him on a secure line after she got settled in her new home to confirm that all arrangements were done or in motion. For his own safety, Anthony swore not to have any contact with her family nor to share any details of his involvement in the case.

Director Vargas had already assigned the agent required to carry out Sarah's escape. Agent Jason was ready but wouldn't meet Sarah until the day of her 'death'. There were many moving pieces and parts to her plan, and it had to all go exactly right over the next two days to be believable. The dominoes were flipping fast.

Chapter 23

Sunday morning meant it was time to watch the 'Angles in Action' bible series with the family. Sarah thought they would object to watching the series, but all she needed was one episode to get her message out and an opportunity for discussion. After the family had assembled and finished the first DVD, Sarah used it as an excuse to ask for comments about angels. The family was perplexed but laughed, recalling some of the movies they had seen with angels portrayed in various funny ways. No one wanted to broach the subject of death, so she introduced it in a nonchalant way, adding that if she died, she would become their guardian angel and leave them all with hints that she was watching over them. So, they had better keep their antennae up to notice her in action! Nervous laughter ensued, so to lighten up the chat, Sarah threatened to haunt Susan and Jackson if their homework wasn't done or if any of them weren't model citizens or if Nicholas remarried a mean woman.

Susan didn't like the conversation anymore and stood up to hug her mom, stating "I know you'll be fine, Mom, because I can't hug an angel."

Sarah swallowed hard, held her emotions back, and promptly switched the subject to getting brunch ready.

Don't look them in the eyes— she thought. *It will give your true feelings away!* Nicholas and Sarah cleaned up the kitchen together and spoke softly while the kids went into the other room to play Monopoly, a game they hadn't played in a long time since it took so long to finish.

"How will you feel about being in the same room as the Kozlovs and their associates?" he asked "It's going to be tense. I think I need to be there for you."

Under no circumstances did she want anyone close to her to be at the hearings or for the criminals to see her family! She knew the agency wouldn't allow it, as it would be difficult enough to protect and transfer *her* to the court building, never mind the others. Still, it was comforting to hear her husband's concerns;

he had been so supportive since the beginning of this ordeal. In the past week, they had talked about their situation almost every day and tried to imagine a time when the criminals were all behind bars and how they could move forward with their lives.

"I'm not going to lie; it will be hard to make it through tomorrow without throwing up or triggering my high blood pressure. My attorneys have briefed me well. I'll be fine, Nic. Don't worry."

Sarah had to keep Nicholas out of the many meetings and briefings, which wasn't easy given how much he wanted to help her. The FBI made sure to keep him out by orders of the director, who knew Nicholas couldn't be involved if Sarah's plan was to work. She knew her faked death would be traumatic for him, especially since his own parents had recently passed, so she jokingly kept the angel conversation going with him a bit longer.

"Nicholas, please don't worry about me. I'm going to get through these next few days and then forget about them for the rest of my life!" she teased. "But seriously, you have been more than loving and supportive during this ordeal. I couldn't have gotten through it without you! But on the slight chance that I choke on a chicken bone or have a stroke, please re-marry and be happy. Just wait maybe two years or so, or I'll have to come back and haunt *you,*" she jokingly said to ease the tension.

He smiled and kissed her, holding her in what would be one of the last embraces of his wife as he knew her. He wanted to be present at the trial, but he knew Sarah, and if she didn't want him there, there was no changing her mind.

As the family retired for the evening, Sarah stayed up once again saying it was to go over her notes, but the real reason was so she could tuck her kids into bed. They all felt it was a bit much, given their ages, but their mom just wanted to reminisce with them and rel-ish memories of their childhood. They allowed her to, knowing how much stress she was under anticipating the trial — and the sweet conversations with their mom allowed them to sleep soundly.

Sarah was to leave the compound early the next morning and just wasn't sure if anyone would be up when she left, so before she turned in, she opened each door once again to gaze on her sleeping family members. Nicholas had fallen asleep watching TV on the couch in his PJs until she woke him up and steered him toward their bedroom.

Finally, when they were all asleep, she quietly went into the bathroom, and with the door closed and locked, she sobbed silently into a towel.

Chapter 24

It was D-Day and time for Sarah to face her first day in court and all that came with it. Max woke her up as if he knew what his favorite human had to deal with. She ate a light breakfast and made sure not to wake up her family as she got ready. She took Max out to his confined plot of grass in the fake backyard to do his duty while she drank her coffee and pretended they were at the park outside the hospital. When they walked back in, the entire family had just gotten up, showering her with much-appreciated good-luck hugs and words of encouragement while still in their pajamas.

"You got this mom, you'll do great, love you mom, when you get back, we'll watch another movie or the angel thing," they all chimed in to make sure she knew they were behind her.

Sarah finished getting ready just in time to hear a knock on the front door. As she left the compound and turned the corner with her escort, she found herself in front of a sea of agents surrounding the area and standing at attention as if they were guarding the president of the United States. It was overwhelming to grasp the scene let alone to be the center and focus of it. Sarah felt like a pawn being told what to do and where to go — what to expect with no time to think about it... just follow and do. And amid all the commotion — an agent stepped forward to help her put on a heavy standard-issue bulletproof vest over her business suit which slammed home the need to survive.

The large squad of agents escorted her to an underground parking area that had six black vans with blackened windows and lights on, ready to deliver their charge to the courthouse. She noticed five other women about her height and size, wearing the same blue suit, getting into the other vans with their agents. The FBI wasn't leaving anything to chance and was employing multiple decoys. The vans all left the secured underground parking area and, with police escorts, headed for the courthouse in different directions. Amazingly enough, they all arrived at the courthouse within minutes of each other.

The courthouse had an underground parking area for just such situations and was prepared to accept the arriving entourage. The motor pool first passed by a corner of the courthouse that revealed hundreds of people and reporters trying to get a glimpse of the players in this high-profile case. Sarah looked with amazement, as she had thought the courtroom would be closed to the public. It was, but people just wanted to be there to see what they could — the gruesome crime and its perpetrators had been widely publicized.

As the motor pool entered the secure garage, it was immediately apparent that it had been cleared of all bystanders. Officers were waiting to form a secure line for Sarah and her FBI lawyers to walk through, surrounded by her security detail. As they all approached the elevators, three of her security guards entered one elevator with her, with three others going into the second elevator and the rest of her detail taking the stairs up the many flights. All moves in and out and around the courthouse were choreographed with her safety in mind. Nothing was left to chance.

As Sarah entered the courtroom and took her seat next to her two appointed FBI attorneys, her blood pressure rose as the Kozlov brothers entered the courtroom and stared at her with their cold eyes. Wearing matching prison-issued suits, they managed to throw out well-timed warning glances her way.

Everyone was in place as the judge entered and started the proceedings by stating the rules and administering the oaths. Lead FBI attorney, Hal Hayden, who had spent many hours briefing and preparing Sarah on today's proceedings, leaned over to ask her how she was doing. He suggested she have some water to calm her nerves, which she needed. Sarah had picked both the Kozlov's out of a lineup and, despite the two-way mirrors, had felt that experience extremely unnerving even though they couldn't see her. Now she was just feet away from them, closer than the night they had tried to shoot her, only this time there wasn't a two-way mirror for anonymity. Sarah felt exposed and vulnerable. As their dark eyes met hers, Sarah saw a cocky hollowness that caused her arms to be covered with goosebumps and her heart to beat faster.

The proceedings began and went on and on with mostly procedural statements and agreements being made until lunchtime was called. Sarah asked what the plan was for the much-needed break and was informed they would adjourn to a nearby office that had no windows and had been cleared by her security detail as safe to use. As the prosecuting team entered the moderate size office, Mr. Hayden walked in.

"Dr. Stevens, sorry for the small lunchroom, it was all we could use given the recent contract on your life."

Sarah abruptly stopped in her tracks, "What contract, Mr. Haden?"

Mr. Hayden looked befuddled. The other agent present tried to stop him from elaborating further, but it was too late. Sarah demanded answers and had a right to know. She knew the odds would be high that a contract would be issued on her life, but she felt her knees weaken when she heard that the bounty was a million dollars! She had to sit down to keep from fainting.

An argument ensued between attorney and agent for the communication blunder, but it was too late, the damage was done, and the cat was out of the bag. Sarah felt like she had been punched in the gut. Sarah gathered her wits about her and reflected on how spot-on she was with her deal. This contract on her life just highlighted the importance of her plan's success.

Sarah tried to eat the sandwich she had brought, but her mouth was too dry, and her stomach was churning. It was tough to forget the piercing stares the Kozlovs had directed her way during court. The indigestion brewing in her empty stomach became too much; she needed to throw up. Sarah demanded to immediately be taken to the bathroom — which the agents quickly complied with. Sarah tried to choke back the stress but found herself sobbing uncontrollably. The agents outside the restroom could hear her sobs and looked at each other helplessly.

The full gravity of the case was hitting her hard. She was walking through the valley of death and knew it would be a rough journey. She grabbed the cross around her neck and said a prayer to continue her walk with Him and asked that He carry her through it. Sarah's faith had carried her before, but for a few moments, she let her maternal instincts take over, causing her to feel empty and scared for her future. She was a strong woman but was totally alone, unable to share the conflict and turmoil within. Sarah had a three-ring circus going inside her head as she tried to rationalize that the ends justified the means… and out in the courtroom — well, it was more than she had bargained for.

Sarah finally gathered her wits and emerged from the bathroom to find her security detail staring at her. She assured them she was ready and asked for a cup of water. The security detail formed their protective circle around her and escorted her and Mr. Hayden back into the courtroom, where there would be detailed questions and a full retelling of the worst night of her life. Sarah was called to the stand and raised her right hand, promising to tell the truth, the whole truth, and nothing but the truth before everyone present in the courtroom.

Both sides took turns asking Sarah questions while the Kozlovs stared intently and tried to intimidate her — throwing cold, glaring looks that could be interpreted as a death threat. She was asked everything from what time she arrived at the office, to what she was wearing, and why she was at work so late that fateful night. Even with all the questions and all the time she spent on the witness stand, both sides agreed they needed more time with her — and requested a second day of testimony. It was a draining experience — one she wanted to forget — but couldn't until tomorrow was over. During her ride back to the compound, Sarah couldn't grasp how an event that took place for just a couple of minutes — could be so complex and take more than one day to recount. It was mind-boggling to think about but also expected.

Chapter 25

That evening when Sarah entered the compound her entire family rushed to meet her.

"How did it go, Mom?" asked Sophie.

"What was it like seeing the thugs in person, Mom?" asked Jackson.

"You OK mom?" Susan chimed in.

"I'll give you a brief overview of what happened today, but that's all," Sarah replied with a smile. "Remember, you can't hear too much about it for your own safety — as well as my nerves!"

"Ok everyone, let's give mom some room to breathe and shake off today," Nicholas guided his wife to the couch to put her feet up.

"How about a glass of wine Hon"? Sarah nodded and without further direction, Jackson took the lead to retrieve the prescribed beverage for his mom.

The family was curious about what happened but had agreed ahead of time that when she returned, they wouldn't pressure her for information if she seemed overwhelmed, exhausted, or appeared to need a positive diversion from the day's experience. Besides, they could ask her more about it after the court case was over, and she felt better.

What the family didn't know was that this was her last night with them, and Sarah wanted it to be special and memorable, not negative, or only about the courtroom experience. Sarah was quiet, dismissing the day's events as trying so she could take in all their conversations and really see and hear her family interact and be themselves.

Sarah listened to every word her loved ones said and tried to notice their every expression as they attempted to comfort and distract her during dinner. Sarah's thoughts and emotions were a whirlwind of conflict and fear. She was distant, but her family just thought she was worn out and tired. Overall, the emotional confusion was accepted as the day's stress and at the end of the evening, Sarah once again tucked each of her kids into bed with their permission and their giggles at the childhood flashback. Sarah then took a long shower and climbed into bed to talk to her loving husband, who was having a hard time staying awake.

Nicholas had been stressed out all day, worrying about what his wife was going through and how she would handle it. There was no doubt that she was both capable and strong-willed, but this was obviously a much more difficult circumstance. He felt helpless to support her. He wanted to ask her about the trial, but she seemed too tired. Maybe she would prefer to talk about it the following evening. So, after seeing her safe return, he provided a healthy family meal and poured one of his favorite spirits. Finally letting his guard down Nicholas immediately felt some tension relief and was almost as exhausted as she was.

So much for her goodbye to Nicholas, Sarah somberly thought, but then realized it was probably best to keep it simple so he wouldn't pick up on her anxiety. Sarah's mind raced in a million different directions as she tried to imagine what would happen the next day. Would she even survive tomorrow, or would the Kozlovs somehow get to her? Would her nerves hold up during her testimony and appear credible? Just how mean would the defense attorney be? Would she chicken out at the last minute? Who would be her assigned agent, and could she really trust whoever they were with her life and ultimately that of her family? So many questions that couldn't be answered triggered an endless loop of worry and another headache. Sarah curled up next to her husband and silently prayed for divine help and sleep. Tomorrow was going to be a complete leap of faith!

Chapter 26

Sarah was up early to avoid any conversations with her family for fear of falling apart and giving away her heart. Her only takeaway item would be her trusty Walkman to hear her favorite songs, safely stowed in her pocket. She took a long look around the room, noticing the remnants of her family's things strewn about.

Hadn't any of them learned to clean up after themselves? She mused. Her mind raced while she rushed through the morning's rituals before anyone else woke up. She had purposely asked to be picked up half an hour earlier than the day before to avoid losing control in front of her family; all she had to do was step outside the door and her fate was sealed.

Then Sarah saw Max, wide awake and standing at the door. She bent down to lavish her loveable dog with the famous Max Rubdown. He returned the affection by licking her face as if to say goodbye to his favorite human for good. She choked back her tears and whispered, "Max, watch over the family for me. I love them and I love you, *so* much!"

Sarah stepped outside of the family compound with teary eyes… she was leaving her life behind and stepping forward into the unknown. A maze of FBI agents waited to repeat yesterday's scripted trip to the courthouse. None of the agents knew Sarah, and she didn't recognize any of them, but she knew that today she would meet the one agent who would hold her life in their hands.

The entourage carefully navigated around the busy city and made good time to the courthouse, with all vans arriving and entering the underground parking area within minutes of each other. The agents were on their toes and delivered Sarah to the courthouse without incident. As they all entered the courtroom, Sarah quickly scanned the faces of those sitting in the courtroom for any sign of Oleg Sokotov. She felt conflicted when she realized that he wasn't in the courtroom and was still at large.

After a brief update by the assigned attorneys, Sarah was ready to face day two of the trial. She nervously watched the Kozlov brothers as they once again entered the courtroom, staring her up and down as if measuring her resolve and size for a coffin! Her focus needed to be on getting the two notorious thugs, who up until now had evaded prosecution, well-deserved life sentences behind bars. Sarah had it in her to see her mandate through — to protect her family — but was walking a thin line of stress just thinking about her future. Sarah quickly slipped the Walkman headphones on to listen to one of her favorite tapes hoping to soothe her nerves before her testimony - just as the judge entered to start the proceedings. Despite her inner turmoil over her fate and future, Sarah stayed focused as she gave her testimony.

"Dr. Stevens, you claimed to have witnessed my clients shoot a man when you were walking back to your office... not when you were in your office... is that correct?" the defense attorney asked.

"Yes," Sarah replied.

"And how is it that you could see the defendants when it was dark and you weren't looking up," asked the attorney trying to throw Sarah off.

"There were hall lights that they were standing under – no one else, just them. When I saw their guns and the victim below through my glass wall - and no one else around- I knew who had fired the guns. It was more than obvious especially when they turned their guns on me and one of them fired!"

"So, you didn't see the defendants actually shoot anyone — isn't that true Dr. Stevens?" The defense attorney smiled. "Had you been drinking that night and… maybe you were confused over what you saw? It was very late."

"Objection," said Mr. Hayden, "Argumentative."

"Sustained," said the judge, to the relief of Sarah's team.

"No, I wasn't drinking. I was working late reading reports and will never forget what I saw or experienced." Sarah addressed both the attorney and the judge with her response. "And I will never forget the sound of those gunshots."

"Could the sounds you heard be a car backfiring? Or a piece of janitorial equipment being used in another office nearby?"

Sarah did not waver when the defense attorneys tried to draw inaccurate conclusions from her truthful recount of the execution she had witnessed. It had been the worst night of her life – she couldn't forget the details even if she tried. The judge was careful to keep the proceedings on track and overruled some of the defense attorney's nonsensical questions. The back and forth seemed endless but Sarah focused, calling up every ounce of energy she had to stay sharp and credible while being questioned by both sides. When her attorneys showed the video surveillance tape that captured everything including the shots fired at Sarah, it was more than obvious the Kozlovs' were guilty and should be convicted!

The legal proceedings for the day concluded with the Kozlovs being led back to jail. As the legal team left the building, her confident attorney Hal Hayden leaned over to state "Your part of the case is done, Dr. Stevens. You did a great job. There will be some technicalities to address to the court, but you can now leave with our gratitude. Your successful testimony today should be the nail in the coffin that puts away these criminals forever!"

Sarah knew she should be just as ecstatic as the FBI team was, but her day was far from over. As the posse of agents organized to escort Sarah back to the van, she cautiously looked around for any sign or clue of what would happen next. She didn't notice anything out of the ordinary, other than Director Vargas stepping forward to congratulate her.

"Dr. Stevens, you were superb on the witness stand!" he said uncharacteristically. "You kept your cool when being crossed examined and even when the Kozlov brothers were staring you down. Excellent job, Sarah. You should be proud of what you did. Your family will be proud of you!"

Sarah had not heard anyone other than Nicholas call her by her first name since the ordeal started, and she liked that acknowledgment, even if it might be the last time she heard it. The two of them walked down the hall with the security detail vigilant around them. With the director present, all were at attention and looking good, going through their practiced maneuvers flawlessly. As the team approached the restrooms, Director Vargas made sure a security sweep had been done for her.

Director Vargas looked directly into Sarah's eyes and suggested "take your time while in there –

relax a bit, you've had a long day."

Sarah looked at him closely for a clue as to what would happen next. Did what he just said have a hidden meaning? Finding none, she automatically followed his advice and entered the restroom to take her time using the toilet. As scared as Sarah was about the unknown, she knew she needed some relief to avoid having the crap scared out of her later. As she washed her hands and ran some cool water over her wrists, she stared at her reflection in the mirror and splashed a bit of water on her face to help calm her. Her senses were on overload and spiked with adrenaline.

Chapter 27

With bladder empty, adrenaline flowing, and poker face on, Sarah slowly walked into the hall to join her security detail and put the heavy bulletproof vest on as directed. The team all walked down the hall in formation, with Director Vargas making small talk with the agents closest to him. As they approached the elevators, he informed the agents that he would escort Dr. Stevens alone in the first elevator, with six agents taking the neighboring elevator and the remaining six going down the many flights of stairs. The protocol was that the elevators wouldn't start their descent until the agents who took the stairs reached the bottom and confirmed that the location was clear.

With the "all clear" signal, the elevator doors were held open for the six agents entering one elevator while Sarah and the director entered the other, both controlled by agents in the building's security room via cameras and verbal commands. Both elevators were monitored by the cameras set up inside.

After the doors closed, Sarah noticed that her elevator didn't move, but she could hear the other one descending, with the agents' loud voices becoming distant. Director Vargas pushed a few buttons to get the elevator going and then looked up to the camera in the corner. He waved at it as if to get someone's attention in the control room to start their descent, but there was zero response.

After a few moments, the elevator lurched downward but then abruptly stopped. Sarah heard a strange popping sound and noticed the director's motor functions start to slow.

"Mr. Vargas, Mr. Vargas…. Are you ok? Has something happened?" Sarah asked nervously, not knowing if this was meant to help or harm her. She quickly looked around for some sort of tool or item to help, but there was nothing.

Director Vargas began to wave his hands wildly and stepped in front of Sarah as if to protect her while looking around for the would-be assailant. Within seconds, he had passed out as Sarah gasped and tried to keep the slumping director from hitting his head on the elevator floor. Just as he collapsed and before she could start her medical evaluation of him, a masked man dressed in black dropped from the elevator roof and into the compartment to face the terrified Sarah.

"I'm your exit strategy," he said coolly. "Items three and four from your Sacrificial Deal. You're on camera right now, so I'm going to fake being the bad guy. Listen and do whatever I say. Do you understand? Nod your head yes and don't talk. Look scared!" Sarah's heart was pounding as she nodded her head. Then watched the mystery man pull a gun out, aim it at her head, and push a button on some gadget from his pocket that controlled the movements of the elevators. He stopped the other elevator, trapping the agents inside, and then started their elevator heading up.

"I want you to look scared and nod your head again," he commanded.

Sarah almost passed out at the sight of the gun pointed at her head and threw her hands up to surrender. Nothing to fake here, she was scared to death!

"You're doing good!" the agent encouraged. "While you're taking off your vest, I'll explain our next moves. Take it off now!"

Sarah numbly obeyed and started taking off the vest.

"We're going up to the roof. I want you to try to prevent me from dragging you to our escape kite, so when we get out, I'll grab you by the back of your blazer, drag you a bit, and then ask you to get into the kite. Do everything I say. I'll be yelling at you, and we'll be on camera, so make it look real! We'll have roughly five minutes to take off before your security detail reaches us. I rigged the elevators, so they won't work properly until someone figures out how to override my commands. It's imperative that we move fast. Do you understand? Get that vest off!!"

Sarah was struggling with the heavy vest. The masked man begrudgingly reached over to help unlatch the confining strap while keeping his gun on her.

Sarah's eyes were larger than ever, but she knew she had to trust the mysterious man – he had said the magic words Sacrificial Deal so he must be one of the good guys… right?

As their elevator door opened to the roof, the mystery man pulled a stick-like bar from the elevator shaft above to jam the door open and render it inoper-able. Next, he grabbed the top of her blazer and dragged Sarah toward what looked like a large, motorized kite. He waved his gun at her, indicating she was to sit in the strange vehicle and put her seat belt and helmet on. As soon as he confirmed her seat belt was fastened, he jumped in and started the engine.

Sarah's once serene world was colliding with the possibility of death as the kite quickly moved to the end of some kind of makeshift runway at the far end of the building roof. Sarah was in full disbelief at what they were about to do—fly off a thirty-story building while sitting in a motorized stunt kite?

No acting was needed—she was terrified, gasping and holding on for dear life as they raced across the rooftop towards the makeshift ramp, gaining incredible speed within seconds. The contraption took off from the roof moments ahead of her security detail, who were breaking down the roof door just as they lifted off. The kite initially swooped down causing Sarah to scream in terror but gained its balance and was now level and airborne, heading southwest toward the Palos Verdes Peninsula. It was an ingenious way to be pulled out of the building! It was almost dark, which gave them cover; however, the agent needed at least a few people to see them when they reached their first destination.

The sound of the kite's engine was deafening, but the agent had thought of that ahead of time and had rigged communication devices in their helmets so they could talk to each other. Within a minute of their takeoff, the agent started briefing Sarah on what not to do while they were flying and what their next move would be at the airport, just minutes away. He also added a few more details to reassure her that he was real and everything happening around her was to make good on the Sacrificial Deal which helped to soothe just a few of her already frazzled nerves.

Sarah managed to look around and noticed the incredible amount of traffic below. *There's no way anyone could follow us through that rush hour quagmire!* She thought. Daylight savings time had already ended – and the late fall air was cold. Flying at dusk at that altitude and speed would have given anyone else a shiver or two, but Sarah didn't feel it. The adrenaline and nervousness had warmed her to the core. The mysterious agent had counted on all of this ahead of time.

"Red Rabbit, are my wings ready? We're ten minutes out – over."

"Copy that Black Bear, we are ready. Out."

Chapter 28

As Sarah admired the afterglow of the sunset fading into almost darkness, the agent changed direction, as if to throw off any possible followers, and headed for the Santa Monica Airport. The agent was busy trying to avoid the LAX jumbo jets flight pattern above them while barking orders to Sarah about the landing and what she would need to do next!

How would they land without being noticed or run over by a plane? She wondered. *And who was Red Rabbit?*

She noticed they were not on a straight approach but came in off to the side with a last-minute maneuver that allowed the agent to visually confirm that they had a clear landing area.

Assuming their movements would be noticed by someone, the agent instructed Sarah to look terrified and to lightly resist him when he pushed her toward a small airplane that would be close to their landing site and truck - and then said something about a wetsuit. She acknowledged the instructions while the motorized stunt kite approached the eastern side of the airport to land. There was a large truck parked with its tailgate open. Their kite landed smoothly and, as it slowed down, the agent tactfully steered them right into the back of the truck. He immediately unbuckled himself and quickly moved to fold the kite's wings up while urging Sarah to get out and take her helmet off.

Both tossed their helmets down and immediately exited from the back of the truck. The agent slapped the side of the truck to signal it to leave. After grabbing Sarah roughly for the benefit of any surveillance – the agent proceeded to push her toward a small plane while the truck sped off, its tailgate automatically closing - as if it had never been there.

Who was driving the truck? Sarah wondered. She was distracted by its movement — *was it controlled by some sort of remote-control thingy as well? Not likely.*

The agent pulled out his gun once again. "Get in the plane," he commanded as he pointed it at her head. Sarah's arms went up involuntarily as she complied and climbed into the backseat next to something large covered by a tarp. She noticed there was some equipment on the floor in front of her and a row of seats was missing from the small plane.

"Put on the headphones and let me know if you see any police or official-looking cars approaching," the agent instructed.

"Oh and put the wetsuit on NOW- you have five minutes!" Sarah didn't hesitate, awkwardly stripping off most of her clothes to put on the oversized wetsuit while glancing up to see if anyone could see her or if others were approaching. The man closed the plane door, jumped into the pilot's seat, and listened intently to the control tower as it barked various instructions to the neighboring pilots. He was waiting for a chance to take off without proper clearance so he wouldn't leave a traceable voice print at the tower. They only waited a couple of minutes before Sarah warned him of approaching lights and sirens. He closed the window, yanked the throttle down, and took off, confident that he could elude the police but not completely sure of the surrounding air traffic. It was another leap of faith!

Flying off a building, then into the darkness, avoiding the nearby LAX jets, and now taking off without clearance from the tower? Sarah had flown in a small plane with her uncle a few times and had always wanted to learn to fly so she intuitively knew they were pressing their luck.

And what is this thing that keeps falling on me, Sarah thought. She peeked under the tarp and gasped at the sight of a dead man whose open eyes seemed to be staring at her! Her heart almost jumped out of her chest at the site of the body's fresh head wounds. A dead man in the seat next to her – jolted by the takeoff – was now leaning on her! She had worked on cadavers in med school, but this shook her to her core, and now she wondered if this masked man flying her around had good intentions or not. Could he be one of the assassins sent to kill her? Or was he really trying to help her? A wave of panic flashed over her as she pushed the dead body off.

The agent, whose face she still had not seen said, "Okay, here comes the next phase of your escape."

Within minutes of takeoff, he put the plane on autopilot and jumped into the back to sit on something behind the pilots' seat, and prepared for the next maneuver.

Chapter 29

"Time to get ready," the mysterious agent barked. He moved quickly, putting the dead man into the pilot's seat, and then dragging a dead woman out from behind Sarah's seat and buckling her into the empty seat next to Sarah. It was now apparent why a row of seats was missing and what the large lump behind her seat had been. There were two dead bodies on this plane!

The man finally took off his mask, but it was too dark to really see his features as he began shouting instructions on what they needed to do next. He took his shirt off, revealing a wetsuit underneath, put on some sort of harness, grabbed her arm to turn her around, and strapped her onto him. It was then that Sarah knew what was about to happen—they were going to jump out of the plane and into the black water below!

He quickly slipped a tracking device over her head, tucked it into the top of her wetsuit, and opened the plane's door.

"We're going to jump out in one minute," he shouted over the rushing of the wind.

"You're doing really well! Take some deep breaths and listen to me carefully. You're attached to me on this parachute. We'll jump out together. When I yell 3-2-1, I'm going to pull a ripcord and release you to drop into the water. When you splash down, pull this cord. It will inflate a life vest that will bring you back up to the surface. I'm going to drop you as close to the water as possible. Keep your legs together and arms crossed, then pull this cord AFTER you hit the water, not before. Do you understand this? Confirm you understand this!"

Sarah numbly nodded. It was all for her family. No time to think, just do.

"Can you swim?" he asked.

Sarah nodded again.

"Good. The life vest will help you out."

Just then the man's watch lit up and started to beep.

"Okay, repeat my instructions verbatim once again," he demanded.

"You'll drop me after a countdown, and I'll

pull this cord after I hit the water." She repeated. "And then do we swim away or what?" Sarah nervously asked as he gave her a nose plug to put on.

"I have a boat that is going to be picking us up," he explained. "Your tracking device is where he'll go to first. Don't worry. You'll be taken care of. Just be sure to pull the cord after you hit the water."

His goal was to get her as close as he could to the water before releasing her. It was now almost dark, making it difficult to ascertain the distance to splash-down, but he had an ace in the hole waiting for him below — the motorized boat had a revolving blue/green light helping to mark the distance to the pick-up zone. The agent had enlisted the help of one of his professional Navy Seal buddies who lived nearby and could be trusted.

His watch went off again, which meant his buddy saw them, and it was time to jump. He quickly rechecked the automatic pilot settings and threw a few items out of the plane he didn't want to be left as possible evidence.

Sarah was strapped to a man that she still hadn't met, had only really seen his eyes, and now was trusting her life to him. Before she could think any further about it, he yelled "JUMP!" The agent put his strong arms around her chest as they leaped out of the plane and plunged towards the ocean's dark surface.

He quickly deployed the parachute. While gliding down with the black canvas below them, the man continued to bark out his orders on how to hit the water safely, how to protect her head, and when to activate the floatation device. Sarah nodded each time and then saw the boat below with the flashing light signaling the waterline. She silently prayed for a quick retrieval.

The boat was getting closer, which meant her time to be dropped was nearer. She could feel the agent's body against her back and appreciated his comforting arm around her chest. She didn't want him to let go – but felt him moving to prepare for her release. She heard him yell, "Keep your arms crossed and legs together. Dropping you in 3-2-1. DROP!"

All he could hear was her muffled scream as she hit the water! Sarah pulled the floatation device cord and quickly surfaced, coughing, and spitting out the water that had filled her screaming mouth. Out of nowhere came the boat with the blue-green light. Two strong arms reach out and pulled her in. Within seconds the mini boat captain maneuvered over to the agent to fish him out and retrieve something else that had been tossed out.

Once the cargo was safely on board, he turned the small, rubber boat to speed off toward the shoreline. The rescuer faced forward, not engaging in any dialogue, simply steering his boat and its occupants toward safety. What seemed like a ten-minute ride ended on a beach in front of an isolated house that Sarah imagined looked inviting during the daytime. It had one tiny light on to mark the way, but not enough to divulge the identity of the approaching threesome.

Chapter 30

Sarah's legs were wobbly, and although she tried to get out of the boat on her own, she fell back landing on her butt. Her entire body was in shock and didn't know how to support her. The man who had flown her off a thirty-story building and then dropped her into the ocean looked down at her, quickly assessing her condition before scooping her up to assist with her walk across the beach and into the house.

The mystery agent pointed her toward the bathroom, "Sarah - take a warm shower and wash your hair, but don't dry it, and don't leave any fingerprints or footprints in the bathroom." He ordered - "Use the extra towel on the sink to wipe them up."

Sarah was shaking from the cold and welcomed the warmth of the shower. Yet she was still moving slowly from the shock of the recent events and proceeded to throw up what was left of the day's meager meals.

"Do you need any help in there?" asked a woman's voice from the other side of the door.

"I think I'm okay," Sarah wearily replied.

Sarah acknowledged seeing the instructions on the bathroom counter. She was to toss all her clothes in a plastic bag and come out wearing new ones that had been laid out for her, including a fabric veil for her face. She was also instructed to put on a pair of clown glasses that had a fake Groucho Marx-type nose and eyebrows in case the veil came off.

As she slowly walked out of the bathroom and into the living room area, she briefly saw the two men who had saved her, one from the water, and the other from the courthouse and plane. The agent was tall and slender but had a rugged edge to his look. The boat captain was also tall and strong-looking, with a kind face that immediately turned away as she entered the room as if to give her some privacy. The woman who had called out to her was rather rotund with several piercings and tattoos. She was wearing a hairstylist's apron and smiled warmly, giving Sarah the feeling that she was in a safe place and in good hands. The woman asked her to sit on a stool that was in the middle of the room on top of a large, paint-splattered tarp. All windows and drapes in the house were closed or covered with brown butcher paper to keep prying eyes from witnessing anything going on within.

As Sarah walked to the stool, the others clapped and complimented her for her bravery and for making it all in one piece. Sarah tried to improvise a clumsy curtsy but almost fell, as her legs were still unstable. She couldn't talk and just stared as the woman guided her to her seat. The unmasked agent stepped forward offering a bottle of water and an aspirin which Sarah silently consumed.

"This won't hurt a bit, honey," said the kind woman. "Don't worry, I'll be gentle."

The woman proceeded to cut off the long, auburn hair Sarah had so carefully cultivated and coiffed since she was a teenager. The woman applied a blond color to Sarah's new crop, being careful not to look under the veil as she worked; it was important to keep Sarah's complete appearance and identity a secret.

After a brief lesson on how to wear the contact lenses that would change her brown eyes to blue, the woman presented Sarah with a mirror and walked away to give Sarah some privacy. Sarah was speechless and just nodded her head, mumbling a weak thank you to the kind woman who had dramatically changed her look to be unrecognizable.

Before she practiced putting in the contacts, Sarah slowly raised the mirror up to see a woman on the verge of a breakdown.

While Sarah was getting her makeover, the men deflated the boat and packed it into an arriving truck along with the parachute, Sarah's clothes, the wetsuits, and all evidence of their presence. The men raked away their footprints in the sand and wiped down all areas where someone could have left a fingerprint. The tarp was the last thing to load up along with the butcher paper covering the windows.

The man in charge made a call, and just like that, it was time to go — *again*. The boat captain and the tattooed woman left as quickly as they first appeared, without Sarah having a chance to thank them. She and her protector drove off in what looked like a large sports car that blended in with the affluent neighborhood. Sitting in the backseat, Sarah noticed a pillow and thought if she could just put her head down for a moment to rest, it would help calm her nerves and stomach.

It was foolish to think that she could stay awake after everything she had been through. She couldn't mourn for her family, because if she did, she knew she would fall apart. Sarah imagined her family huddled together, crying, asking questions, and confused as to what had happened to her. She worried about her kids, Nicholas, and even Max, waiting for her to come home.

She was very much in shock. Luckily, the melodic movements of the car rocked her into a deep sleep, surrendering her fate to a man she still had not properly met, but was forced to trust with her life.

Chapter 31

In what seemed like only minutes later, the mysterious man was trying to wake the exhausted passenger, repeatedly shaking her arm, and gently calling her name so as not to scare her. As she started to come to, she hoped to open her eyes to see Nicholas but instead saw her protector through the blur, with his blue eyes being the first thing she focused on. All at once she was startled and shook violently in fear.

"It's okay, Dr. Stevens," he said while reaching out his hand to help her out. "We're at a different airport. Your flight is ready. It's time to go."

He began wiping off all possible fingerprints from the car handles and backseat where the Doc had slept.

Blinking from the light and still groggy from the deep sleep Sarah reached back to take the pillow with her. Her protector had the same idea and the two bumped heads. Sarah begged for forgiveness and fell backward when he released his arm from hers to rub his head. It was an awkward moment for both, but he was quick to grab both the pillow and Sarah to keep the mission moving forward – to get her on the private jet. It was obvious that this wasn't a regular airport – she wasn't even sure where she was. After Sarah was secured in her seat facing the back of the shiny-white jet, the agent knocked on the cockpit door to give the OK signal to take off.

Sarah sat directly across the seat from agent Jason and for the first time got a good look at him without a mask and gun. His dark hair, blue eyes, gentle facial lines, and voice made him seem about the same age as she.

What a relief to be assigned to someone experienced and not out on his first rodeo! She thought. As she sat silently looking at him, he took the cue to introduce himself in a most amusing but professional way.

"Hi, I'm Jason. I will be your official escort for the foreseeable future," he said and extended his hand out with a somewhat serious look to put his charge at ease. She reached out to shake his firm hand and stared at him with her tired eyes, still in disbelief at what she had just been through and still groggy from the deep nap in the car.

"I must say, you set the bar pretty high with that agreement and willingness to go through what you did," continued Jason. "You did great on all that I put you through! I read your file and studied your past and present activities and determined you would make it — and you did!" He smiled warmly.

"That was the physical part of your journey," he assured. "We will now take two flights tonight, both on privately issued FBI jets. The pilots won't see you, and you won't see them. The second set of pilots was hand-selected by me to take you to your destination, which I have also selected. No one at the agency will know where you are except for me. In the unlikely event of my death, you can call FBI Director Vargas, for guidance. He's the only one who knows I was assigned to your case."

"In the file, I've prepared for you," he continued, "you'll find your new ID, your new address, and all relevant facts you need to know about your *new past* should you be asked. The rules of your new life are outlined, and you'll need to memorize them before going outside your new home. You and I will run through them one more time before I leave you. I'll give you my phone number to memorize should you have any questions or concerns after I leave." Jason passed her a water bottle. "Here! You need to drink some water. Your body needs it!"

Sarah complied and took a sip. But she remained silent. She was still in shock and didn't have much energy to do anything other than listen to his instructions.

"I know you're probably wondering what happened to the plane we were in," Agent Jason continued. "It crashed by one of the Santa Barbara islands. I wanted people to think your captor was headed back with you in the plane to collect on the contract that was issued on your life. The dead guy I put in the pilot's seat was a newly deceased contract killer who would've wanted to collect on you. The woman was about your size. We made sure her dental records matched yours, compliments of a recent break-in at your dentist's office. It's best you don't ask who she was or how she ended up in the plane."

Sarah took a deep breath, surveyed her surroundings in the plane. "How and when will my family be told about my death?" she asked.

"Your family is safe and was just notified of your accident," Agent Jason said, as he relayed the details, being careful with the words he used and watching her reaction as he spoke.

"They have started their mourning process. Dr. Stevens, you delivered in court for us, so we will now deliver for you!"

Sarah shook her head to indicate that she heard him. She wanted to cry but just couldn't. She didn't have any more energy or emotions left, so she just shook her head up and down with tears welling up in her eyes.

"Okay," she replied meekly. "Were you the one who orchestrated those things we just did?"

"Yes," Agent Jason confirmed.

"Were there any agents hurt in the elevator?" she slowly asked. "Or how about Director Vargas? Will he be okay?"

"Yes, he's fine, though he may have a bit of a hangover from the drug on the dart," Jason replied.

"And where are we going, where will I live?" she managed to mutter under her tired breath.

"You'll see!" he exclaimed. "And I think you'll

like my arrangements. Please open your file up and start reading, *Sandra*!"

Chapter 32

The time went by fast, and somewhere in the middle of nowhere they landed and parked next to a similar plane inside a large military base-looking hangar. Agent Jason tapped the door to remind the pilots of the rules and protocols regarding this transport. Just in case, a large blanket was tossed over Sarah's head as she deplaned one aircraft and boarded the other. Both planes took off, one right after the other, but headed in different directions. The second crew was handpicked - trusted former military buddies of Agent Jason - and were handed their flight plan minutes before takeoff. They promptly adjusted their instruments to accommodate what the tower needed to know for takeoff.

Sarah tried to read her file but couldn't stop thinking about her ordeal and didn't have the focus to absorb what she was reading. Her mind was racing with a million questions with her body somewhat paralyzed by the exhaustive events. Mostly she wondered how her family was holding up. As she surveyed the plane, she noticed the window shades wouldn't open and were permanently stuck closed.

Was this plane used for cases like hers? She wondered for a moment and then tried to restart reading the file stocked with rules on what she could and couldn't do while in the Witness Protection Program.

The plane landed late at night with no one around at a small airport.

Where was she? Agent Jason made a quick call to someone asking about the conditions outside and whether there was any unusual activity. There were other exchanges, but she couldn't hear and really didn't try to. The plane taxied to an area at the far end of the runway and slowed. To Sarah's amazement, Jason opened the hatch while the plane still had some forward momentum - commanded that she immediately deplane by hitting the ground and rolling out of the engine's danger zone!

After Sarah numbly complied, Agent Jason tossed two bags out of the plane, pounded three times on the cockpit door, and then jumped, rolling toward Sarah. The door automatically closed as the plane taxied down the runway for another textbook takeoff, leaving Agent Jason and Sarah sitting on the tarmac – bags scattered about. Both walked to a parked car nearby, tossed their stuff in, and drove off. Sarah was again wondering what would be next – was there something wrong that caused them to jump out of the plane like that??

"OK – that's it, no more physical stuff – you are home – no more flights just a quick drive and it's all over," Jason promised.

After several minutes they drove up to a house near the end of a cul-de-sac. Sarah noticed that everyone else's lights were off except the neighbor next door, who had a light on upstairs. Agent Jason opened the house's garage door with his remote, drove in to park next to a Honda Civic, and had the garage door closing behind them before the car was even turned off. The whole thing was well thought out and orchestrated by Agent Jason from start to finish. Sarah took a deep breath, feeling that the ordeal was about to be over and the spinning in her head starting to subside.

As they walked upstairs into the house, Sarah noticed that it was sparsely appointed. It kind of looked like the previous occupant had been a bachelor, or at least it was decorated as such. The house had three bedrooms upstairs suitable for a small family and kitchen and living area downstairs. It looked like someone had stocked the kitchen for Sarah with her favorite foods, and immediately she wondered if Agent Jason had entered the FBI compound home while the family was out at Disneyland to do some recon work on her. Maybe the competent Mrs. Mueller had given him some tips, but how could she? No one was to know of his involvement in this case.

It looked like he had thought of everything, including the headache meds. Not bad! He showed her to the master bedroom and tossed one of the unknown bags from the beach house on the bed for her to go through. It contained some of her own clothes and toiletries, but mostly she was happy to see a Walkman fall out of the bag.

"I took the liberty of making a copy of your music," said Agent Jason. "I heard you loved your Walkman, but I was afraid that yours wouldn't survive the trip, so I made a duplicate tape."

"How did you know which music I liked or had on my…? Never mind," Sarah mumbled. Her thinking wasn't clear. Of course, he could do that — he was in the FBI!

"Why don't you get some rest?" Agent Jason suggested. "I'll stay in one of the bedrooms for the night. I'll just be an earshot away if you need anything."

Sarah was happy that she didn't have to think. Her mind was numb. She had just entered another world and didn't even know where they were! Dutifully she turned around to go back into her room.

"You really did well today, on all accounts," Agent Jason added. "Straight across the board, you were exceptional!"

Sarah smiled wearily at the compliment as she closed the door behind her and the life she had once loved.

There would be no more familiar routines for bedtime, for work, or for interacting with her family. She had died tonight and would be imprisoned for an unknown amount of time to deal with the aftermath.

Alone, Sarah climbed into the new bed and began to sob uncontrollably from deep within her soul as she tried to process the day, mourning herself, her family, and life. She cried herself to sleep, with Agent Jason nearby hearing her sorrow and powerless to help.

Chapter 33

Could this have been a nightmare? The only way to find out was to get up and see for herself. Sarah had slept soundly for twelve hours and awoke hearing Agent Jason politely knocking on her bedroom door calling out for Sandra. Reality sank in. Yesterday *did* happen. And who the heck was Sandra? Sarah began to rise, but not necessarily shine, before realizing that *she* was Sandra. It was her new name. She had approved a list of names, and Sandra had been one of them.

She looked out the window and wondered where they had ended up. The weather looked chilly, there was a green lawn out front, and the other homes looked fine. There were even a few kids playing out in the street. She was in a suburban neighborhood that reminded her of Santa Barbara.

As Sandra, she put on the thin robe she found in the closet and walked downstairs to find Agent Jason sipping coffee from a large mug.

"Is there any more of that around?" she asked him, wishing for good news and noticing the coffee pot behind him still half full of the much-needed wake-up juice.

As she drank her coffee, Agent 'Jason on It' started going over his checklist. He halted when he saw her sunlight-lit silhouette from the patio door. He tried to be polite and not look as she moved to the other corner of the room, slowly surveying her new environment as she walked around. He was relieved when she finally took a seat at the kitchen table.

Slowly, he restarted his list of the rules and regulations, watching her reactions to make sure she heard and acknowledged them along the way.

"Agent Jason, I was top of my class and chief of pediatrics in Santa Barbara!" she snapped. "I'm sure I can read your memo and understand it."

Right after the words left her mouth, she was embarrassed and apologized for her sarcasm. The coffee had kicked in, and her brain was now fully engaged, though her skin still had remnants of the previous night's dunk in the ocean, all topped off by a slight headache.

"It's okay, Sandra," he responded. "And you can just call me Jason. As hard as it may seem, you need to practice your new name and life story. Repeat all this over and over, even out loud, to ingrain this information until it becomes a natural reality. Don't go outside until you're prepared – but you do have some nice neighbors on either side of you. Remember that you are renting this home from a man also named Jason, whom you've never met, and probably won't."

"Now, it's time for me to leave and for you to start your new life, Sandra," he patiently continued. "Your new bank is called First National Bank of Boise. A check will be deposited to your account on the first of each month." He handed her an envelope.

"Your ID info is in this envelope, along with the third copy of your agreement to deposit into a safe deposit box at the bank. You know we couldn't comply with item number 14 of your deal – you know the one about traveling out of the country? So please stick around..." Jason smiled, looking for a supportive glance. "But I did manage to get you a new Walkman– remember – last night in your bag?"

Sandra gave him a small smile back and thanked him for the gesture. Now she knew where she was—Boise, Idaho! She had never been to Boise, let alone Idaho. *So, this was it*, she thought, *her new home.*

Jason finished his instructions. "I hope to call you soon to let you know about your first secret family observation," he said. "It'll be at a date and time of my choosing. I'll keep you posted."

As Jason walked toward the door with his overnight bag in hand, an immediate rush of 'don't leave' overcame her. Her protector, the only person who knew that Sarah still existed, was about to disappear, leaving her alone. Her anxiety level went back up as the door closed, and she realized he was gone and the house quiet. The lack of sound was unnerving. She was instantly lonely; left on her own to start a new life when she should have been enjoying the one she had carefully built and nurtured with her husband and family.

Chapter 34

As Day Three in court was about to end, a messenger delivered a note to the bailiff who, in turn, delivered it to the judge, who read it in somber silence. After the counsel for the FBI had finished questioning the Kozlovs, the judge cleared his throat and then read the note's contents out loud. The people in the courtroom gasped as they learned of the death of Dr. Sarah Stevens the night before. A few outbursts of emotion sent the room abuzz, which the judge had anticipated. A few of the Stevens' friends who had been approved to attend the trial broke down in tears at the news.

The Kozlovs' defense lawyers were privately elated and without hesitation called for the case to be dismissed. The judge quickly denied the request on the grounds that Dr. Stevens had already taken the witness stand and had given her testimony under oath. She had completed the cross-examination by the defense, and everything was recorded. He wanted this case to go on and was going to see it to its conclusion. The judge slammed the gavel down as he delivered his decision.

The Kozlov brothers were relieved to hear the news of Sarah's death at first, but she had already delivered her blow to them during the first two days of testimony. They had issued the million-dollar contract on her life just days after the crime occurred—and from behind bars, no less! Who did the job and why wasn't it done before her appearance in court? The Kozlovs had wanted her dead, and now they wanted the details and proof. Their greedy side surfaced when they pondered if the act of killing Sarah was done too late for the contract to be collected on. As the brothers prepared to leave the courtroom, Pavel Kozlov leaned over to one of their attorneys and privately whispered....

"I want to know who completed that contract and all the details," he commanded in a low and almost-inaudible voice. "I want proof that this is real. Use all our available resources on this. And I mean *all*!" His attorney nodded and looked around nervously to make sure their conversation had stayed private.

Chapter 35

Sarah, who started calling herself Sandra to get used to her new name, was now on her own. She was in a new house that needed some serious decorating help. But more importantly, she was alive, and her family was now safe, though in mourning.

Sandra walked around the house, opening cupboards, and surveying her new digs. The house was quiet and really had no life, no personality; it felt like it just existed to provide a roof over her head and nothing more. She headed upstairs – the squeaky floorboards sounded off and it was apparent they needed some TLC…. as did the wooden bedroom floors… all creaky. She numbly showered and dressed using clothes from the bag Jason had left for her – she didn't care what it was until she passed the long mirror in the hallway and stopped to stare at the stranger in the reflection.

For the first time in many years, she really looked at herself and her body. Flabbiness and extra weight had slowly taken over her once athletic build.

There hadn't been enough time to take care of herself the way she should have. She had neglected herself. She had looked after her family, patients, the new pediatric wing, but not herself. She had always been the last one in line for her own attention and care, and it showed. Mostly, she stared at her new look and mourned all that she had lost.

As Sandra, she would have lots of opportunities to put herself first and strive for a healthier reflection both inside and out. She had been athletic in school but having three babies and a crazy work schedule had taken its toll on her. It was now visible through the stranger who solemnly stared back at her in the mirror. She was taken aback by the look and tired expression her reflection revealed and decided not to look at a mirror again for the rest of the day.

There was a lot to process and think about, but mostly there was hope. For the time being, hope would keep her alive and sane. After she learned more about *who* she was from the file Jason left for her - it would be time to get out and explore Boise.

Chapter 36

Sandra carefully re-read her dossier and, as Jason had suggested, read her newly assigned identity out loud several times. She would need to sound convincing as Sandra, so she practiced. After she felt a bit more comfortable in her new identity, she went upstairs to change.

The clothes Jason had picked out for her showed that he had zero taste in women's clothing! A trip into town was needed to open her bank accounts and find out where the shopping centers were for clothes and groceries. And maybe, just maybe, she would investigate taking a self-defense course, something she had always wanted to do but never had the time or motivation to do it as Sarah. Given the recent events and circumstances, there was no time like the present to start. But not today. She was still groggy from her death.

The Honda in her garage seemed to come with the house. Luckily for her, it had a Thomas Guide map book sitting on the passenger side – with the page open to where she lived, and address written in margins in case she forgot. *Was there anything Jason didn't think of?*

She drove off, taking in the details of her street and the houses on it, hoping to recognize them on the way back. Next door, an elderly couple sitting on their porch and enjoying the early afternoon waved to her as she drove off. A family across the street looked like they had three boys under the age of ten. Farther down was another family with younger kids.

This was her kind of neighborhood, she thought. Sandra looked forward to meeting her neighbors once she got settled. Right now, she was still in mourning – with the loss of her family too fresh and raw to deal with meeting new people. She would need some time before confidently engaging with others. Best to practice on those she would not be seeing again.

It was a nice ride. The surrounding mountains looked like the ones in Santa Barbara, but taller, more rustic, and sprinkled with light snow. It would be nice to take a trip up to see them – but not today. Today was about getting her banking set up and picking up supplies. Sandra knew that the overall weather in Boise would be a bit more extreme than what she was used to in Santa Barbara, but then again, anywhere else would have temperatures fluctuating more than her picturesque hometown.

Boise was also just far enough away from Santa Barbara to keep her from jumping into her car for an unapproved road trip home, but close enough that the FBI-approved transport could get her home within a reasonable amount of time for her secret visits. Here, she could blend into the large city from the outskirts, minutes from the highway and another few minutes from the airport she hoped to be flying in and out of once Jason arranged her first visit.

Chapter 37

Sandra managed to get her bank accounts opened and find the mall and a gym before deciding to call it quits for the day and drive home. Sandra was still emotionally drained, tired, and her eyes were still puffy from crying herself to sleep. As she pulled into her driveway, she noticed her elderly next-door neighbors still sitting outside so she gave them a friendly wave. They took this gesture as an opportunity to meet their new neighbor and walked over to greet her.

"Hello, young lady- welcome to the neighborhood," stated the older man with a smile on his face and arm outstretched to greet Sandra. "My name is Harold Bennett, and this is my wife Martha."

"Pleased to meet you both," replied Sandra and shook their hands with a smile back.

Harold and Martha appeared to be in their mid-to-late-70s. Martha was portly and had the satisfied look of a woman ready for her well-earned afternoon break. She was wearing a comfortable but older tea-length dress and had her shiny, gray hair up in a bun.

She seemed friendly, approachable, and ready to meet her new neighbor. The lines on her face showed a warm and caring demeanor and a voice that could put grandbabies happily to sleep.

Harold looked like he had been both a dock worker and drill sergeant in his earlier years. He was shaped like a mini tank, sported a 1960s buzz cut, enjoyed his retirement, and showed it by wearing his long-sleeved shirt long and loose. His handshake was firm and his voice steady and friendly.

The Bennett's appeared to be a happy, settled, and stable couple. Sandra didn't need any more drama in her life; she was looking for slow and steady and was pleasantly surprised at an invitation to come over for afternoon refreshments and small talk. She cautiously accepted the invitation and chance for a diversion.

Sandra loved how friendly and parental the Bennett's seemed, making sure their guest was comfortable and had enough to eat and drink. Martha kept offering her the remnants of what was the moistest coffeecake Sandra had ever tasted. It was divine and had just enough of a drizzle of chocolate sprinkled over it to satisfy any sweet tooth.

"Martha, your coffee cake… is amazing, so moist – when did you make it?"

"Just made it this morning- Harold has a sweet tooth that can't be fixed – can you tell?" Martha replied with a funny grin that continued to put Sandra at ease.

Sandra made the small talk needed to be polite but remained guarded in how she answered Martha's questions. When asked about her family and where she had moved from, Sandra swallowed hard and spoke slowly, using memorized details from the dossier Jason had prepared. Tears welled up in her eyes as she spoke about losing her family in an accident and then asked to not talk anymore about it. Sandra had become nervous and couldn't make eye contact with the sweet couple –

Would they see through her and know she was lying? Thought Sandra. *Could she keep it together?*

Harold came to her rescue and declared the interrogation over.

"We offer our sincerest condolences, " he said, "Given your circumstances, it's probably a good idea to add a little something with a kick to the lemonade to welcome our new neighbor!"

Sandra smiled and politely declined the alcoholic addition for fear of losing control. She needed to keep her wits about her and knew she was a lightweight in the world of liquid spirits. She quickly remembered one of Jason's suggestions for diverting attention.

"Please tell me about your family!" She said.

Harold and Martha shared that they had two sons; the younger one was married and had two kids; the older son was newly divorced with no kids. She could see the disappointment in their faces as they talked about the older son's recent divorce but seemed optimistic that he would eventually settle down and find the right woman. Harold had been a career military man with Martha raising their two boys; both were happy to not be moving from one military base to another anymore!

As she walked around looking at their photos, Sandra noticed none existed of their oldest son.

"We're getting new ones without his ex-wife in them!" Martha quickly replied.

Everyone laughed, and Sandra knew these dear people would be wonderful neighbors to get to know. After goodbyes were exchanged, Harold and Martha hugged her.

"I insist you come over for dinner tomorrow for my specialty—lasagna!" said Martha.

"A home-cooked meal sounds delish!" Sandra replied. "I accept, but on one condition—that I bring either a salad or a dessert or whatever is needed."

"Anything with chocolate suits me!" Harold exclaimed.

"I have to admit to being a bit of a chocoholic myself!" Sandra said with a smile. "I'll bring a chocolate dessert as my contribution for the dinner."

After another round of thanks and hugs, she walked out for her thirty-second commute home. Sandra reflected on the evening and fondly remembered her parents, who had both passed not too long ago. They had had her late in life, which wasn't the norm at that time. She had been an only child and had enjoyed growing up with their full attention and devotion. They were her number-one fans and great role models, but both had died within a year of each other. Her father died first of a heart attack, and her mom died soon after, literally of a broken heart. They were in their eighties and were a part of their grandkids' lives, and left their daughter secure in her own heart that she had been loved. She missed them dearly but was relieved to have spared them from witnessing her death.

Sandra got the feeling all was okay with Harold and Martha and their place in life. As long as they didn't try to play matchmaker or ask too many questions, she would be comfortable spending time with them – helping to fill up the holes in her heart.

Chapter 38

It was still slow going each morning. Sandra missed her morning wake-up nuzzle from Max, the lively family breakfasts, and rushing out the door for whatever the day would bring.

Now, when she first woke up, it was quiet, with zero activity happening downstairs. It was a solitary existence. No one needed a ride, breakfast, a walk, or would call her into the office to take care of a patient. It was all about her now, with no accountability to anyone. It was a strange and unfamiliar world to her of being alone and nonexistent.

She still felt groggy from the emotional trauma of secretly saying goodbye to her family and the never-ending adrenaline rush she endured from her escape. It had all happened so fast, and now life had come to a screeching halt, forcing her to start over. Sandra had never had so much time on her hands —ever! When she was finishing school, she had already been married and had started her family. She could run a household, be a mom, and study for med school at night when the kids were in bed. Every hour had been filled with too many things to do, which she had thrived on and handled like a pro. Now she had no calendar to glance at hourly and nowhere to be. It was an unusual and empty feeling to not be needed by anyone.

What she really missed most was Nicholas and their intimate moments; stolen times in between all the chaos they had called their life. She dreamt of her and Nicholas cuddling and spending time together on a Saturday morning doing nothing before they started their weekend. Feelings of regret at not spending more time with him or being more intimate sporadically surfaced and sent her into a dark mood laced with guilt and blame. She tried to avoid these types of thoughts but would lose the battle after seeing couples out and about together – smiling, walking, sharing a meal…. any of these encounters painfully reminded her of what she had and lost. Her new life left an unseen hole in her heart that would take time to mend – if it could. As she stared at herself in the mirror, she hoped it would talk back and give her guidance.

Sandra made breakfast and sat down with a piece of paper and pen she found in a nearby drawer that held miscellaneous items and was now deemed the junk drawer of the house. Every home had one, and this one was no exception. The blank paper mirrored how she felt about her new life - empty. What should she do? Should she get a job? If so, where? What could she do that involved kids without her identity and experience being discovered? Part of the agreement with the FBI stated she was not allowed to be a doctor – but maybe something related to her training? Sandra was a blank piece of humanity needing to be filled in with a new purpose. There was enough income from her deal to live off - but she couldn't just allow her days to be empty when they were once filled with meaning, purpose, and joy. Surely, there was something out there for her. It was time to figure out what that new purpose would be here in Boise.

Leading up to her escape was the single thought of saving her family. Now she could focus on the provisions of the Sacrificial Deal – the thought of this whole new existence being a temporary stop toward the bigger goal of one day being reunited with her family. She didn't know how long this would take but knew the possibility of her freedom existed if the

Kozlov brothers and Oleg were either behind bars or dead. She needed to hold onto that thought every single day as part of her inspiration for getting up and living in the present while still mourning her past. Her life just veered off course -headed down some detour - without knowing when she would get back on the path she had been on.

As Sandra took another long look in the mirror, one thing stood out as a no-brainer move—making the time to get herself healthy and back in shape. Whether or not she liked the idea of this life change was immaterial; those were the cards she was dealt and would deal with. Sandra would capitalize on this unplanned opportunity to do something about it with the same gusto and perseverance she had needed to get through med school while pregnant.

After a lot of thought and a tall glass of water, she took pen to paper and began scripting her foreseeable future. She called her list 'The New You!' As one of those overly organized types, Sandra liked to write down her obligations, goals, and other important items to not only remember them but to help make them happen - a constant reminder to work towards. This would be similar, so she created her list with the same thoroughness and careful thought she had recently given to her Sacrificial Deal – without the pressure. Her New You! list became her commitment to make lemonade out of the lemons she had been given and to preserve her sanity.

Chapter 39

THE NEW YOU!

My Prescription for Me

1) Workout five days a week at a gym. Hire trainer so I don't kill myself the first few weeks. Keep trainer afterward to continue the program and push myself harder. Take before photos (neck down) for inspiration but keep private.

2) If I do #1 right, should lose 30+ pounds and tone up. One year to get this done.

3) Try to avoid chocolate to help with #1 and #2!

4) Look for employment or better yet, part-time/volunteer work that involves kids. Kids probably won't ask a lot of questions about my past. Cannot hang around hospitals, or other pediatric-related practices, for fear of being discovered due to their state licensing requirements. Was told not to do this by Director Vargas.

5) Find out what grows around here and plant a garden. Always wanted to grow my own fresh

fruits and veggies. Add mature fruit trees if room/possible. Go organic?

6) Take self-defense classes, maybe even go for a black belt in karate if not too old. Need to learn how to protect myself — just in case.

7) Learn how to shoot a gun. I'm afraid of guns—dah! By the looks of it, I'm in the right state for this! Take classes?

8) Plan out first secret observation visit to be Susan's graduation - lots of people will be there. Binoculars will be needed, practice my makeup disguise skills. Is there a theater program at a local college to help with this or I could intern somewhere to learn? Are there even interns for this kind of stuff? If Jason calls me… ask him to make this the first visit.

9) Learn how to cook? Take classes, but who would I be cooking for? Maybe do later or find class on how to prepare low-calorie meals? Maybe use as place to meet people?

10) Fix up this house! Looks like an unhappy bachelor lived here. Needs color, house is dreary looking, brighten it up. Take decorating class?

11) Get stereo and other music/cassettes I love for Walkman.

12) Find a church and go on Sundays. Ask God for help in staying calm, finding a new direction, and going the distance with this new life.

Writing and adding her thoughts to The New You! list felt as if Sandra was self-diagnosing and prescribing her own cure. It was exhausting trying to think of it all and it took a couple of days to finish, but she was a detail-oriented woman trying to think of everything while on a mission to a new her. She knew her list was missing an important part of her life but thought it best to leave her love life off it for now. She had hoped to someday be reunited with Nicholas when this ordeal was over – she would never forget him and deeply held onto that possibility of picking up right where they left off, even though deep down she knew it might be impossible. How would he know to wait for her? Another leap of faith.

It was time to implement her new game plan. It was time to seize the opportunity for improvement - staying busy had worked to keep her kids out of trouble - so it could help her as well… diversions to curb the loneliness… Failure to distract herself could be physically and emotionally devastating. It was time to turn lemons into lemonade, and if she had liked alcoholic drinks - she would have even made it a lemontini!

She jumped in her car and opened the garage door to pull out slowly and carefully, the way Agent Jason had taught her to do so for safety reasons. With a map of Boise by her side, she was out on her second adventure in her new hometown, looking for an organic grocery store and other healthy places to support her new game plan.

No time like the present to start, she thought. The distraction would be therapeutic and just what the 'Doc' had ordered.

Chapter 40

"Dang!" Sandra yelled at her trainer. "That workout just about killed me!"

The five days a week commitment was a tough routine to get used to – not to mention the constant muscle soreness that plagued her since day one. Working out had seemed a lot easier when she was younger - but her determination won out. After all, showing up was 90% of the success equation. So, she did – week after week despite her body's protest.

The daily workouts also helped relieve the residual stress and anxiety she still felt; the ordeal she went through had jolted her entire body and was akin to being in a car accident. The healing process just took time.

Another stumbling block was learning to shoot a gun. Sandra had broken down in tears both times she had taken lessons. She found it difficult to point a gun at the target dummy hanging from a clothespin fifty feet away and the blaring sound of the gun discharging its bullet was felt throughout her body. The flashbacks of that fateful night were still freshly ingrained in her memory.

An obstacle to overcome, she silently confessed to herself. Sandra knew it would take time to heal those wounds and since she had plenty of time, she would be patient and put in the work.

Winters in Idaho meant very cold weather. It was still too chilly to plant a garden, but not too early to start planning for one. Sandra began making a lot of trips to the local nursery to get books about what she could plant, the best times to plant, and what amendments would be best for the soil in her backyard. She also started buying the tools needed to help make it all happen.

Sandra started scouring weekend garage and estate sales to find things to make the house she now lived in homier.

How do you turn a house into a home? She asked herself. *When do you know it's a home and not just a house?*

Sandra hoped she would learn the answer. She missed her home in Santa Barbara and had loved its layout and the local help in keeping it beautiful. Reflecting on her past life, she appreciated the gardeners and their housekeeper Claire that had helped the Stevens family enjoy their home. Sandra wished she had thanked them more for their commitment to them.

Mostly, Sandra missed Nicholas and the comfortable and safe relationship they had. It could take years for this 'deal' to play out and for her to be free from the self-imposed prison she was in.

Would Nicholas wait or remarry unaware that his wife was alive and waiting for both him and justice? The thought of resuming a future relationship with Nicholas and seeing her family again kept her going. For now, hope was all she had.

Chapter 41

Some months later, the big day arrived. Jason would be showing up to take Sandra away for her first secret family observation in Santa Barbara. She was thrilled to no end. Her daughter Susan was graduating from high school, and Sandra was going to be there to witness it—in disguise.

Her daughter had always wanted to be a veterinarian and had designed every bit of her life so she could be around her furry friends by interning for local vets whenever she could. She loved learning about animals and focused on dogs as her main priority. At home, she had been the main family member to take care of Max. She brought him to her tennis practices as the tennis team's unofficial mascot. She had even brought Max on group dates which unnerved a few of the young men who wouldn't dare invade Susan's personal space for fear of upsetting the protective Max. It had been her dad's idea that Max go on the group dates. *Clever Nic!*

Sandra was certain Susan would be accepted to UC Davis's Veterinary School, given her stellar GPA and experience interning with the local vets who promised glowing letters of recommendation. Being in Idaho and unable to speak to her family, she felt so distant and disconnected from their lives.

Did Susan receive that coveted acceptance letter or did the dramatic events derail her chances? Susan had been so much like her mom, with her tenacity and intuition. There was something in Susan's young being that allowed her to observe the world around her in great detail, noticing things that most would miss. An important life skill.

That would serve her well in the medical world, thought Sandra, *whether it be with humans or animals.*

Susan's graduation day had been at the forefront of Sandra's mind since she had first penned the Sacrificial Deal. All she could think about in the week leading up to the secret visit was what it would be like to see her cherished family again – if even at a distance. The theater classes she had started taking in Boise would prove helpful in keeping an even keel and maintaining her fake persona; a good test of her resolve upon seeing her family for the first time in months.

Jason had called her several times to prepare her and review the plans for the trip to Santa Barbara. They discussed many details like how they would use the FBI-issued plane to get to the Santa Barbara Airport and when she would put on her makeup and disguise.

She would be dressed as an older woman roughly in her eighties and was even briefed on how to deplane as that character, using a cane and a slightly hunched posture. Jason would be acting as her son, so he could stay close to his 'mother.' Nothing would be left to chance as they discussed the details and possibilities. She would remain safe, and ultimately would keep her family safe, by being meticulous and thinking about every possible detail and scenario.

Sandra agreed that it would be a good idea to keep a distance from her family and anyone else who could recognize her. More importantly, she was supposed to stay silent, for fear her voice might be recognized.

Sandra was under no illusion about how serious the consequences could be if she failed. She prepared by repeatedly practicing 'what-if' scenarios in her head. She even went to a thrift store and asked for help in buying a dress for her 'grandmother' who Sandra claimed was about her size. Jason would bring the wig and glasses; Sandra would bring the rest of the disguise. She was determined to be ready for the big day, and even put a small pebble in her shoe to remind her to limp a little bit!

She was nervous. Jason had let her know that Oleg Sokotov was still at large, and there hadn't been any leads on his whereabouts.

Chapter 42

Jason arrived at her house right on time. He drove straight into the garage and made sure it closed behind him before exiting the rented car. As he walked through the back door and into the kitchen, he made sure to loudly announce himself to avoid scaring Sandra. As he turned the corner, he found her sitting at the kitchen counter with a big smile, excited for their day. As she stood up and walked around to greet him, Jason was caught off guard by her transformation. He hadn't seen her since the ordeal began but was overwhelmed by her slenderized, curvy body and her big smile.

He quickly cleared his throat and asked, "Can you show me your disguise?"

"Oh, well hello to you, too!" she replied. "I thought you might like some iced tea or something before we left?"

Jason realized the importance of his charge feeling confident about her day ahead. He had taken an early flight to get to Boise that morning, and though he wanted to follow the rules of the deal, he also knew the risks they were taking. Primarily, he was worried about Oleg discovering her secret!

As an extra precaution, Director Vargas had assigned undercover FBI agents to be at the graduation to protect the Stevens family – as well as to look out for Oleg Sokotov. None of these agents knew that Sandra would be there in disguise or that she was even alive. They didn't even know that Agent Jason would be there. The agents in attendance would also be in disguise while watching for Oleg. If he was present, he would probably be in disguise as well. It was a lot to navigate for the experienced Jason, but nothing could deter Sandra from this day.

After more prep talk and her impromptu modeling of the granny disguise, they got into Jason's rental, opened the garage door, and drove off to the airport. FBI protocols called for the car to go to the far end of the hanger and park behind the plane with covered windows. Jason called to confirm they had arrived at the airport, giving the pilots the go-ahead to close the cockpit door for privacy and start their pre-takeoff checklist.

Once the hangar door closed Sandra emerged

from the car wearing plain clothes, a long coat, and a large scarf to cover her head. She would change into the granny outfit and do her makeup once they were on board. They needed to make sure that the pilots didn't see her, and Jason instructed her to take the seat facing towards the back of the plane in case a pilot needed to use the bathroom. Once everything was in place, the hangar doors were opened for the plane to taxi and take off.

Chapter 43

The last time Sandra had been on the plane with Jason she had been in a state of shock. Today, she was in control of her emotions, though very excited to be headed to her ol' stomping grounds, if only for a few hours.

The jet was nice, with comfortable seats that felt like they could convert to flat beds for longer trips. The galley was well stocked with snacks and beverages, but she was too excited to eat and didn't want to risk messing up her make-up or disguise.

After the plane took off, Sandra quickly grabbed her makeup kit and went to work transforming her face to that of one thirty years her senior. All the theater makeup classes she took, along with research, were proving helpful to keep her identity shielded. Jason casually watched Sandra as she skillfully used her makeup tools, as he imagined she had done previously with a scalpel and stethoscope.

Sandra's long-sleeved dress and gloves pretty much covered her up; she used a pearl necklace and earrings as the finishing touches for her elderly look. She was ready to go long before he was.

For his disguise, Jason sprayed some gray hair dye to age his look before adding a fake sparse-looking beard. He put on an outfit that would have been suitable for teaching a college-level history class on the East Coast. His tweed blazer, glasses, and cap were a 'smart' look for him. They would fit in well at the graduation and disembarked from the plane with confidence. They hailed a cab. A short ride later they entered the chaos of graduation excitement and a sea of excited families anxious to see a diploma presented to their children.

Jason exited the cab and dashed over to open Sandra's door. He extended his hand to help her out, with Sandra briefly feeling as if she was exiting a limo to attend the Academy Awards. She would be acting today!

As she stood, she was careful not to completely straighten up and remembered to use her cane while holding onto Jason's outstretched arm which was what any properly raised son would do for his aging mother. Nervous but hiding within her character, she appreciated how steady Jason was, guiding her to a section of the bleachers that would give her the best view of the festivities. He had scouted the location out and knew how important this day was for Sandra and to get them a good seat.

Both slowly walked together with Sandra's left arm holding his and her right arm on the cane. As they took their seats among the other families, Sandra looked around and recognized a few faces. They had had no idea who she was. They were giddy, and probably all thinking about the parties lined up afterward to honor their graduates. Jason secured a program and gave it to his 'mom' to read. As she anxiously scoured it for Susan's name, the festivities began with the traditional Pomp and Circumstance played by the school band with an added twist of jazz. The crowd cheered as the graduates filed in from their hidden spot behind the school gym to take their seats.

Sandra finally spotted Susan's name in the program and immediately noticed that the school where she would be attending was not UC Davis but in fact was the local UC Santa Barbara.

What had changed? Did Susan switch her major or did she not get accepted to Davis? These were questions that would, for the time being, go unanswered. As Sandra looked up, there was her daughter walking toward the student seats, all smiles, with lots of decorations on her cap and sporting what looked like a Hawaiian lei. Nicholas had always said he would fly one in for her, just like he had done for Sophie and Jackson when they graduated. Sandra had to remember not to sit up straight and beam with pride at seeing her daughter looking so confident; instead, she squeezed Jason's arm.

Jason responded coolly with a nod and kept his gaze vigilant around the perimeter to see if he could spot any of his colleagues. The four FBI undercover agents were easy for him to pick out due to their attentive nature, their shoes, and their uncommunicative posture with others around them. Jason was glad they were there but had to keep Sandra under their radar— no sudden clapping when Susan's name was called. She was there only to observe. They had rehearsed this.

When Susan's name was called to receive her diploma, Sandra just squeezed Jason's arm and lovingly gazed at her daughter, who was now a full-fledged young woman with a bright future ahead of her. What

Sandra didn't anticipate was the outburst of cheers and support the school poured out for Susan. When the story of her mother's death had been released, the community had stepped up to surround the family with meals and support both at school and at home. It was heartwarming to hear the applause, but there was an even louder group within the stands who stood up to cheer her on. It was the Stevens family, as well as her cousins, aunts, and uncles, their neighbors, and friends all standing to support Susan! Even Max was there barking for her! Sandra kept her excitement in check and lovingly watched her daughter receive her diploma while the crowd cheered her on!

Sandra felt strained. She could glance over at her family but couldn't stare or hold her gaze on the ones she longed to hug. She knew the rules and was hoping to linger in the stands after the ceremony to get a better look at them all. Jason had whispered his approval because after all - old ladies needed more time to move.

Jason felt her take a long, deep breath as she squeezed his arm with a contented sigh. It was time to leave the ceremony gracefully and get into the waiting cab that Jason had paid extra to guarantee a quick ride back to the airport.

As Sandra and Jason walked towards the exit the Stevens family changed course and headed toward the same exit just past where they were seated. It was like a small family mob heading towards them, and there was nothing that she could do about it but keep to the side of the bleachers to allow them all to pass. She had a great disguise and was thankful for her dark sunglasses, hiding her tears at being so close to her family and her old life, but unable to truly be a part of it.

The Stevens family filed past them, chatting about where the party would be and waving to Susan below, who was hugging her friends. Not one of them thought anything about the elderly woman with a cane and her son that they politely passed by.

As Nicholas walked by, Sandra looked up at him, noticing his quiet demeanor and hollow eyes. Although he had a slight slump in his posture, she noticed he stood up a bit taller when he saw his baby girl ahead. Sandra ached to jump into his arms but reminded herself that she was protecting them by staying back.

He looks so distant but is right there – I could reach out and touch him, she thought. He had been through a stressful ordeal that had obviously left its mark on him. But he was holding it together for his daughter. *God, she missed him.*

Things were going as they had rehearsed, and the family didn't notice her - but then she saw Max! Jackson strode right past his mom with Max on the leash, but as the two passed by each other, Max stopped and whined, lurching forward toward the familiar scent of one of his favorite people - someone he had missed and didn't understand why she was missing or why she was gone! Jackson looked a little surprised but kept Max from running off.

Maybe the old lady and her son had a treat in their pockets? Max whimpered and glanced at the old woman as she kept walking, still trying to follow her. Just then, Susan popped up onto the bleachers to see her family, and the family's attention turned to her. Max kept whimpering and testing the leash. Susan noticed Max was out of sorts and tried to see what was bothering him. She looked around briefly but could only see the backsides of the crowd exiting the bleachers to find and hug their grads. It wasn't long before she was distracted by well-wishers with congratulatory smooches and 'atta girl' high fives. Max continued to whimper as he saw his Sarah leaving. He would never forget his Sarah!

Chapter 44

As Sandra and Jason climbed back into the safety of the FBI jet, she finally managed to straighten up her posture and twirl with excitement at having pulled off her first visit! She was all smiles at seeing not just her immediate family but extended ones and neighbors who had put a supportive cocoon around Susan. When she was Dr. Sarah, Sandra had always volunteered for classroom activities, such as driving kids on various field trips, supporting sports teams with medical help, and serving as the go-to mom when a neighbor's child was sick or injured. It was comforting to see these same folks paying it forward by keeping Susan supported. She imagined them doing the same for Jackson. Sophie, thankfully, had Austin to lean on.

What more could Sandra want other than to find out what happened with Susan's vet-school plans? No matter. Susan was going to UCSB, and that was a success in and of itself for her to stay in school.

"Did you see Susan and her honor ribbons?" she asked Jason energetically. "That was my baby girl and she looked great"!

Jason nodded and allowed her to marvel in the moment. He complimented her on following the rules and staying in character but had his 'Let's review what we just did' hat on.

"Max almost gave you away," he said carefully. "Good thing Susan was distracted. She's a smart cookie! Under normal circumstances, she would have followed up on what was bothering her dog."

"You're right," Sandra proudly agreed, "She is a smart cookie."

Both were silent for a moment, hoping that no one had noticed Max's interest in them at the graduation. Elated as she was at having been able to see her family, she couldn't stop thinking about Nicholas' distant eyes when she had walked past him. He looked older. The ordeal had aged him, and she wondered how he was handling his new lifestyle.

She missed him… She missed everyone.

The plane took off and as Sandra changed back into her street clothes in the restroom, Jason's mind was racing.

How should he improve the next visit? What might he

want to do differently, and what might Sandra see next?

As Sandra finished dressing and returned to her seat, her smile had disappeared. She had a somber look as she stared out the window. She realized it would be another six months or so before she saw her family again, and that was only if Jason could find a public place to do it. She played the day's festivities over and over in her mind.

Jackson looked good—taller, even! Sophia and Austin were holding hands and seemed happy. Her niece looked like she was sporting a nose ring, Max looked healthy and attentive -But Nicholas's eyes... She couldn't get those eyes out of her mind. He had withstood the worst of the ordeal, worrying about his kids and losing his wife. Nicholas had to make and accept a lot of changes; his face and eyes told the somber story.

Chapter 45

Jason dropped her off at the house in Boise via the protocol of driving into the garage first, then closing the garage door before exiting the car. They also had a way to tell if the garage door had been tampered with, along with checking the other doors into the house. Jason had trained her to be vigilant with her own safety, and she had become adept at practicing what he had taught her and what her self-defense teacher had instructed. He stayed in the car as she got out.

"We did great today!" he joked. "Really, you did well! I'm tired, so I'll be heading back. You okay?"

She turned around.

"Yes, son, I'm good," she replied with a weary smile. "And you looked good for your role today. Thank you for an incredibly special day. I'm grateful!"

"Okay, Mom," Jason replied as she turned to head into the house. "You looked good too! I'll call you soon."

She waved back and noted it was the first time

Jason had smiled *and* paid her a compliment.

It really had been a great day!

Chapter 46

Thanks to the testimony of Dr. Sarah Stevens, the Kozlov brothers were incarcerated causing their connections to run for cover, wondering if the two brothers would rat them out to shorten their time behind bars. Because of their ties to the outside world, the brothers knew Oleg was still on the lam. If he was caught, they knew he could cut a deal to disclose the crime family's illegal holdings to save his own butt from jail time. If that happened, it could be the end of the Kozlovs' business empire – even while in jail.

Therefore, Oleg was now being hunted by both the authorities *and* the Kozlov family, and so far, had been successful in evading both!

Oleg had never found any proof that Sarah had died since no one stepped forward to claim the completed contract on her life. And if she was alive, she still posed a threat to his freedom - so he continued to pursue his own investigations into her whereabouts.

In complete disguise and pretending to be a part of another family he purposely sat next to, Oleg had been at Susan's graduation. He did notice Max's odd behavior but couldn't see who Max's attention was aimed at. Still, he saw enough to keep him interested in further stakeouts of the Stevens family as he wasn't completely sold on the doctor's death and how it happened.

Dr. Stevens had already testified against the crime family but if Oleg was ever caught, she could once again testify against Oleg. He wanted to be sure she was dead. Oleg knew the Kozlov's businesses well and had been a faithful lieutenant to them for years, but now it was his turn to cash in. If he could confirm that Dr. Stevens was dead, he could step up and take over the Kozlov empire. He needed that proof and would see to it personally to get it or do the deed himself.

Chapter 47

Sarah's new life as Sandra was going well - but it wasn't fulfilling. She accepted that fact and tried to make the best of the hand she had been dealt, but for now, she wanted that happy feeling of seeing Susan's graduation to last like a well-crafted, slow-burning candle. She savored that visit and would dole out the warm memories throughout the next few months whenever she needed a boost of energy or felt alone.

She smiled when she thought of Susan walking into the stadium with her cap and gown all decorated, her head held high, waving to her supportive family and friends as they cheered. Sandra smiled, remembering how she had walked past her big family without being discovered! It gave her hope for the next visit.

What would she see and when?

It was all up to Jason. On-site agents sent their reports on the Stevens family for review to Director Vargas. Little did they know that those reports were passed along to Agent Jason when Vargas thought it was important for him to know the particulars of the family's plans or issues. Jason was playing both sides of the fence by being the secret connection to Sandra and being a part of the FBI's other business units. It was a juggling act he did well. The Stevens family only knew the agents personally assigned to them and not who the agents reported to.

Director Vargas made sure Jason was never assigned to be near the Stevens family for fear of them recognizing him during one of the secret visits. Jason's role had become more like that of an inside double agent who played for the same team but at different positions, without the other team members knowing. Somehow, he made it work.

Chapter 48

Sandra continued with her new life, working out, taking karate lessons, practicing at the gun range, and working in her garden, which was now producing food safe enough to eat. She enjoyed her new neighbors and despite Jason's concern had taken a part-time job working at the front desk of a pediatrician group that specialized in serving kids with developmentally challenged physical issues. She knew it was risky to work there, but she needed to have some way to remember her old world and loved seeing the kids come into the office. There were a few times she thought that she had accidentally exposed too much of her experience as a pediatrician. She explained her slip-ups as due to having other family members in the medical field and claimed to have worked at their offices during her school breaks when she was younger. She even made sure to carry a medical book to work to make it look like she was studying something related to her job. This worked with her bosses, who believed they had hired the best administrative assistant ever, with no one the wiser to her identity or background!

During some of her lunch breaks, Sandra would take a short walk outside, pretending to have Max by her side, like when they used to head to the hospital to make their rounds. The memories made her smile while her part-time job gave her the much-needed joy and feeling of usefulness she craved.

It had taken some time to find the right karate program, but when she did, she felt good about her Sensei and his abilities to teach her the self-defense ropes. There were times, when feelings of helplessness flooded her during the lessons – thoughts of Oleg coming after her and what he would do to her if he found her.

Sensei Roberge surmised that she'd had a previous bad experience. He had been instructing for over 25 years and was used to fragile women coming in with the hope of being able to stave off future problems with their new-found craft. The reality was quite different, but the confidence they gained was priceless and would serve them well in most situations. He instilled in his students the ability to use good judgment to avoid trouble, not seek to destroy it. The Sensei initially handled Sandra with kid gloves, but over time slowly took them off, and pushed her into more difficult moves to challenge his highly motivated student.

What Sandra really looked forward to was showing Jason her new gun range skills. She figured, given his profession and background, that he must be a good shot. Perhaps a friendly outing to the local shooting range could be entertaining for them both? She still needed lots of practice before she could have a shoot-off, but she loved the idea of working toward this goal. Despite her circumstances, she was a woman on a mission to self-correct her course. It was a slow process.

Sandra was moving forward, punching the proverbial timecard of life in hopes of one day earning the big bonus: her old life back. It was not guaranteed to happen but she wanted to be ready for whatever came her way and prepared accordingly.

Chapter 49

It had been two and a half years and three secret visits so far, keeping the flame of a hopeful future still burning inside Sandra. She still kept up her workouts, visited the gun range, worked her garden, and kept her life as busy as she could to pass the time quickly. Sandra liked to sit on the bedroom window seat gazing out into the cul de sac to watch the neighborhood kids playing a game while the parents talked and did their weekend chores. It was a nice life they all seemed to have and one that she missed with her family.

It was why Sandra loved spending time with Harold and Martha next door as they gave her a feeling of being safe and accepted without a lot of questions being asked.

Jason called to let Sandra know that they would be leaving the next day to attend her cousin's wedding. It would be held in the city of Hermosa Beach, right on the shore. This would give them a chance to hide in plain sight with the public and observe from a safe distance. The reception would be in a nearby restaurant that they obviously couldn't go to but at least she could view the ceremony with all her family expected to be in attendance. The beach was a perfect venue to blend in at, and she would once again dress to look like Jason's mother. The anticipation gave Sandra an extra bounce to her step as she got ready.

The wedding was to start at 5 p.m. to allow for a near-sunset ceremony. The timing was great for photos but not so good when trying to shield one's face from the direct sunlight. Nonetheless, there would be plenty of beachgoers to hide among while observing the ceremony and its guests from a safe distance, so the day was a go.

Sandra had found a pair of binocular type eyeglasses that allowed her to see people better at a distance while keeping her distance. With a newly styled wig and dress picked out - she was ready to go. She never wore the same dress twice and made sure her 'old lady' look was different each time.

Jason arrived the next day on time and was greeted by an eager Sandra that had to show off her look for the big day before he could get a word in about the day's schedule and rules to follow.

"So what do you think, son? Do I look old enough? Sandra quipped.

"Yep, I think you're getting the hang of this." When he looked at his charge, he had to admit, her makeup and overall disguise prep were getting even better.

"Let's go over our checklist and backup plans before we take off. I'm thinking you might need a light shawl as it might be cool at the beach – isn't that something old ladies wear?" Jason sarcastically said to get a smile out of Sandra. She went along with his schtick but agreed, knowing the shawl could also provide an even stronger disguise.

They reviewed their checklist of what to do and say like two pros at a debate. They arrived at the airport following all the safety precautions, like where to park in the hangar, how to move from car to plane while covered up, and where to sit once on board. It was becoming a more comfortable routine. The expected van with darkened windows and normal-looking license plates awaited them at the airport in Torrance to get them to the beach.

The beautiful late spring day was sure to please the beach-going admirers. A light breeze and temperatures in the high 70s ensured the guests' and wedding party's comfort, as well as those in disguise. By now, the Stevens family had felt it was no longer necessary to have FBI protection 24/7 but did continue that coverage during the evenings so that they all felt secure enough to sleep. They had opted not to have security for this day trip to Hermosa Beach, which was great for Jason; he wouldn't have to worry about his colleagues discovering him. Still, he maintained his attentive eagle-like gaze, always on the lookout for any sign of Oleg.

Chapter 50

As the old lady was ceremoniously being helped out of the van with her cane, Sandra breathed in the fresh ocean air with a sigh. She loved the beach and being there gave her a momentary flashback to the many times she and Nicholas had taken their kids to their nearby beach in Santa Barbara. There were many barbecues, parties, and neighborhood events at the beach with the kids all running around having fun. Jackson surfed, and both Sophie and Susan played beach volleyball with friends. Sandra remembered it all, including trying to get the beach tar off their feet due to that area having one of the largest natural oil seepages in the country. Today, she would only admire the wedding proceedings and not the tiny tar-stained feet of yesteryear.

While enjoying the familiar scent of a California beach, she reached out for Jason's arm to steady herself while keeping in character. Sandra was surprised to see so many people at the beach at the late hour but understood how the power of a beautiful day at the coast could bring people out. Jason had parked the van a good distance from the wedding area so they could slowly walk by at just the right time to see the festivities begin from The Strand (the cement walking and bike path). He would call the shots today: their speed as they walked by, deciding whether there were enough bystanders gawking to allow them to stop and blend in or, for whatever reason if it wasn't safe, to stop and head back to the van.

They were lucky today—there were lots of people on the beach walking and biking on The Strand. It would be easy to walk near the back of the ceremony area while keeping a safe distance and not be noticed. As the wedding guests arrived and mingled about, her high-powered glasses revealed the Stevens family approaching and being greeted by the other guests on the sand.

Sophie and Austin were getting lots of attention, mostly directed at Sophie's stomach. She must be pregnant! Judging by the small but exaggerated bump, it looked like this future grandbaby would be born in about five months give or take. Sandra looked up at Jason with questioning eyes remembering she was not allowed to talk for fear of someone recognizing her voice.

He leaned over to ever so slightly whisper in her ear, "I was wondering if the great Doctor 'S' would notice. Yep, she's due in February!"

Sandra let out a tiny, inaudible sigh of delight and squeezed Jason's supportive arm hard. As she took in that historic moment and zoomed her focus at the future Grandpa Nicholas for his approving eyes, her happy moment stopped when she noticed an unfamiliar woman on his arm. Whoever she was, it appeared that Nicholas had been with this woman long enough to feel comfortable enough to invite her to a family wedding. The mystery woman appeared to be about the same age and height as Nicholas, had long dark hair, and was nicely dressed. The other guests warmly greeted her as if they had known her for a while. The Stevens family chose to sit in the same aisle together, along with *that* woman.

The sight of seeing her husband with another woman was too much for her to bear, and tears streamed down her cheeks. Sandra did jokingly tell Nicholas that if anything happened to her, he should remarry but to wait at least two years. She knew this would be the right thing for him to do. After all, to him, she was dead. But the reality of seeing him with a new woman still sent an arrow through her heart. She gasped for air while trying to keep her emotions in check. Seeing her Nic with another woman at this wedding was just too much!

Sandra motioned for Jason to start back toward the car. Today's visit would be a short one. She had seen her family and friends and witnessed her daughter's joy in telling others about her future baby. But that was all Sandra could handle without losing it in public.

Jason had known Sandra would eventually find out about Nicholas's new love but didn't know he would be bringing her to the wedding. Without hesitation Jason got Sandra into the backseat of the van and, once in with the door closed, Sandra let her guard down to silently cry. Her hope that she could return to her life - and have it be just like before - was gone. Sandra had held onto the hope that maybe her exile would end before her husband found someone else. That glimmer of hope had helped her get through some dark days at the beginning of her new life. The hope of being reunited with her family – even if many years out - gave her a will to move forward… to get up in the morning ... but now it was obvious that her husband had moved on.

Chapter 51

Jason didn't say anything to Sandra during the trip home until they were on board the plane and he was asked the question he knew he would get.

"Did you know about the girlfriend?" Sandra inquired.

"Yes," he replied slowly.

"They have been together for about a year. I'm sorry for not telling you sooner, Sandra, and this may not be the best time to share this, but…." Jason took a deep breath to find the right words to say…. "Nicholas proposed to her last month. They will marry sometime next year."

Jason knew she was hurt and thought it best to get it all out now, to allow her the chance to put it all behind her once and for all. He just didn't get women and how to handle them very well, which probably explained why his only marriage ended in divorce. He had wanted to marry, settle down, and have kids, but his job was so demanding and sent him on similar missions around the country that he just couldn't explain to his girlfriends or wife. He missed important events that were viewed as him not being attentive to the relationship or caring enough, hence the several breakups and one divorce under his belt.

After delivering the bad news and seeing the faraway stares and silent tears stream down her cheeks, Jason retrieved a box of tissues from the plane's restroom and offered it to her. Her eyes were red and swollen, with the remnants of her makeup job dripping onto her thrift store dress. He felt bad for her and knew she'd handled more than her fair share of losses during the short time he knew her. This woman had endured and grown stronger, but part of her sanity had been tied to hope—hope that she would exit the self-imposed exile and rejoin her family and marriage. Now the marriage part was officially over.

Sandra rationally accepted the facts, but her heart was not in alignment with her head, knowing now that any future she might have with her family and new grandbaby would be without Nicholas. She hoped that Sophie was in the care of her godmother, best friend, and business partner, Dr. Kathy. Sandra still had something to look forward to.

As Jason pulled into the garage and lowered the door, he felt bad about delivering the day's rotten news and thought he should hang around before leaving.

"You know, I'm kind of hungry," he said casually. "How about I order in something from the pizzeria in town? Are you hungry?"

She felt a bit surprised by the suggestion and felt she had little energy to do much of anything, but she agreed to the idea.

"Sure," she said with the hint of a smile. "No anchovies, please."

She was tired but wanted the company of someone who knew *her*— and not her fake persona.

Jason took her response as a good sign to stay a bit longer. They had already become confidants and with all the time they spent on calls and planning out the visits, they were now slowly becoming good friends. He made a quick call to the pilots who would be waiting for him and then the pizzeria but needed to know….

"Hey Grandma," he smirked, "do you want some salad with your pizza?"

Sandra knew he was trying to cheer her up and

nodded her head in agreement with a side of smile.

Chapter 52

Several months later and Jason would need help to cook up something elaborate and special for the visit to see the soon-to-be-born grandchild. Sandra had waited for the big day like a kid waiting impatiently for Santa Claus. She insisted she help with the planning of this so-called 'mission,' as they would be treading on her familiar turf: her hospital in Santa Barbara. A reluctant Jason conceded and allowed her to assist with the logistics. Many hours were spent on the phone, along with a personal visit from Jason to hammer out the details while reviewing a set of building plans he got from the Planning and Development Department of Santa Barbara.

He reminded his eager co-conspirator of the consequences of not following the plan or allowing her emotions to show during the critical parts of the visit. This somewhat dampened the mood, but perseverance was all she knew these days. She liked the idea of helping to execute this plan. And to think it would take place at the very hospital where her three kids were born and where she had visited her patients with Max by her side!

For her look to be believable by her former colleagues and any hospital visitors who might see her, she needed her makeup and clothes to be believable once again as an elderly woman. By now, she had perfected her skills and would do her best work on herself for this important visit. *Every* visit was important, of course, but in this case, she would not be outdoors where she could blend in or observe from a distance. Instead, she would be close to her targets and would need to go unnoticed or risk giving her identity away.

The stakes were high, but she knew every hall they would be walking down and where every restroom was just in case, she needed to duck in or quickly disappear. She knew when the shift changes occurred, which orderlies were observant and which were slackers, and how to find out where Sophie's room would be. She had thought long and hard about this visit and had left no stone unturned when it came to the details she shared about her former world and the protocols each employee followed while on duty in the maternity ward.

Jason appreciated her knowledge of what and where they would be going but was realistic and apprehensive about the risks. There were too many parts to their plan that could go south. Without the necessary multiple escape routes, he was used to having access to, not to mention the security cameras pointed at them, he was concerned.

Jason finally called one early evening in October to announce that their plan would be implemented that night, as Sophie had just delivered the new grandchild! Like an expectant mother-to-be herself, Sandra had her bag, wig, and accessories already packed and ready to go at the front door. She would have only one chance to see Sophie and her grandbaby at the hospital, and nothing would get in her way of a successful, secretive visit to anonymously see them both.

Chapter 53

Knowing the hospital like no other, Sandra had to instruct Jason on how she would avoid the admittance office and greeters. The goal was not to deal with anyone, instead to go directly up to the maternity ward as if visiting a granddaughter and babies, all wrapped and snuggled in their bassinets. If that didn't work, she would keep her voice in off mode under the auspices of having laryngitis or just being old and slightly off wanting to see the babies. If questioned and needing to speak, she would do it in a whisper to keep all within earshot from recognizing her voice. Jason would act as the concerned son and pave the wave to communicate for her if needed. Either way, they would secretly leave through the side door when done. Security cameras were everywhere, Sandra would need to keep her head lowered the entire time. Jason's taller frame would be difficult to blend in, so he would have a detailed disguise that included a hat and thick glasses to help.

After multiple discussions with Director Vargas, who vehemently opposed the trip for fear of the twosome being caught, he finally gave the stamp of approval. The day had come, and nothing would keep Sandra from this visit!

As she left the plane, she noticed the wheelchair at the bottom of the stairs and sat down to test it out. Jason had outfitted her ride to look the part but had hidden a weapon in it, just in case. Sandra had some patients over the years who were wheelchair-bound, but she had never navigated one herself until now. Jason's job was to push her around in it, so they both practiced their roles and shared pointers, which provided some much-needed comic relief in the privacy of the large empty hanger.

As they approached the hospital, she was surprised to see that nothing had physically changed. None of her plans or recommendations had been implemented, so her knowledge of the hospital's layout was still good. Still, she wondered why nothing had been done to start the new wing of the hospital she had spent so much time designing with Kathy. Her thoughts were interrupted by the realization that it was late, and they needed to get up to the maternity ward before the visiting hours were over.

Lucky for them, by entering like they owned the place and with Sarah's knowledge of where they were headed during the shift change, no one asked them to sign in or engaged in any dialog. The tall man pushing his 'mom' in the wheelchair looked like they belonged.

As the elevator doors opened and they exited into the maternity ward, goosebumps hit Sandra's arms as she recognized most of the staff. Fortunately, she looked like a regular visitor being wheeled down the hall by her son to visit the babies. Jason knew where to navigate to by the taps of her fingers on the wheel-chair's armrests. Fingers tapping on the left side meant to turn left; right side, turn right. Index finger pointed forward meant walk straight ahead, and fist closed meant to stop.

They successfully arrived at the maternity ward's viewing window and saw the babies all tucked into their bassinets. It had been a busy day, with what looked like some 20+ babies all lined up for a night of interrupted slumber that would include feedings with their new mothers, diapers changed, and routine health checkups. It took her only moments to pick out her grandbaby with the name, Sarah Ann O'Neill, attached to the pink bassinette. The parents' names were also listed: Sophie and Austin O'Neill.

Sandra lovingly gazed at her brand-new granddaughter and marveled at how quickly the baby had been named. Blushing at the loving thought that Sophie had honored her with that name, she squinted to look at the time and weight stats. Baby Sarah was born just hours ago and was doing great! She looked up and saw her best friend Dr. Kathy Mitchell across the room who had been staring at them since they had arrived at the window.

Kathy had assisted in delivering Sandra's granddaughter as Sophie had politely requested of her Godmother early on in the pregnancy. Kathy had been sitting for her first break all evening, thinking about how special it was to have been present for the birth of her deceased best friend's grandchild when the mystery couple appeared at the viewing window. It was a late hour for an elderly woman to be out Kathy thought, noticing her gaze was aimed at baby Sarah.

Those proud eyes seemed familiar to Kathy. She knew all the members of the Stevens family but not these two. The more Kathy looked at the older woman, the more she was drawn to find out who she was and finally walked around the hallway to meet her.

Seeing her dear friend headed her way, Sandra gave Jason the emergency sign to leave, but before he could steer the wheelchair around, Kathy quickly came around the corner.

"Hi, folks," she politely said in a loud voice to get their attention. "Would you like to see the babies up close?" Kathy kept her eyes on the old woman for any sign of family recognition.

"Oh, no thanks," Jason responded. "We're done now. I need to take my mom back home."

"Which baby were you here to see?" Kathy prodded.

Kathy's intuitiveness in asking the right questions and being able to correctly diagnose her young patients had always impressed her former business partner now sitting in the wheelchair. Kathy wouldn't give up her inquisitiveness until she was convinced she had all the right answers, and for some reason, she felt compelled to learn more about these visitors in the maternity ward.

Kathy kept asking questions and just when Jason was about to answer, the old woman in the wheelchair sneezed loudly. That was all Kathy needed to know who was really sitting in the wheelchair in front of her! The hair on Kathy's arms went up and triggered an immediate reaction to grab and inspect the old lady's arm before she could pull it back.

To Kathy's surprise, she confirmed her suspicion as correct and saw the presence of a scar they both had due to a late-night climb over a rusty fence via a dare during med school. That scar was on her wrist! Kathy gasped while covering her mouth to suppress her surprise at the positive confirmation that this woman was her best friend, Sarah!

Chapter 54

After Sarah's signal Jason quickly decided to leave the hospital and said, "I'm sorry, my mom isn't feeling well, I need to get her back to her room," while turning the wheelchair around to escape.

Kathy gave a barely noticeable nod and wink to her BFF and grabbed the wheelchair from Jason while stating in her commanding voice, "The restroom is down the hall sir. Please let me take your mom to it. We'll be right back."

"My mom's okay," Jason protested. "She doesn't need a break!" and reached out to take back the wheelchair.

"Oh, you know it isn't right for a son to have to deal with his mom's bathroom breaks!" Kathy said in her authoritative voice, keeping control of the wheelchair and nudging Jason away with a smile. Before Jason knew it, the two women were behind a locked restroom door! Kathy turned around to see her old friend firmly standing straight up from the wheelchair with tears of happiness in her eyes.

"Sarah, is it really you?" Kathy cautiously asked while staring into the woman's eyes. "Please say yes to confirm that I'm not dreaming or seeing a ghost!

"Yes, yes!" Sarah whispered and tightly hugged her old friend while trying to gain control of her emotions. But she soon lost that battle as the two started firing questions at each other, excitedly talking like two schoolgirls who hadn't seen each other in decades.

"Shh!" whispered Sarah. "We have to be quiet! No one can know who I am! I only have a few minutes to talk!"

The two of them chatted, with Sarah asking about her daughter and sharing information about her self-imposed entry into the Witness Protection Program to save her family.

Jason was pressed up close to the bathroom door and could hear voices and serious tones of conversation flying back and forth. As a nurse walked by and was ready to ask Jason what he was doing, he bounced back into character and knocked on the restroom door.

"Mom, you okay in there?" he asked to appease the passing nurse with the inquisitive eyes.

Within seconds, Kathy popped her head out and exclaimed, "She's constipated and will need more time," before quickly slamming the door shut, knowing she had just bought a few more precious minutes with her dear friend. Jason knew the secret had been exposed and was powerless to change or control the unscripted next moves of these two women.

Sophie had been one of Kathy's first deliveries into the world all those years ago. She had become an honorary aunt to Sophie and loved seeing her come in with her mom over the years to learn what they did for other kids under their care. Now, Kathy had personally made sure that Sophie had taken good care of herself during her pregnancy and was prepared to be a good mom. Sophie was now officially her first second-generation patient!

Kathy shared the good news of Sophie's uncomplicated delivery and suggested they quietly sneak into Sophie's room to see her sleeping the busy evening off, which Sarah thought was a good idea and had to be the one to softly articulate it to Jason upon emerging from the bathroom with a coy smile.

"Jason, this is my good friend and former

business partner Kathy, who I'm sure you know has figured out who I am." Kathy proudly nodded in agreement while slowly steering the wheelchair down the hall while all talked softly.

"She knows the story but swore to keep it confidential – and I know I can trust her with my life" Sarah stated while looking straight into Jason's eyes. "She knows my daughter is asleep and said I can go and observe her for a few moments from a dark corner of her hospital room."

Jason was visibly worried about her breaking the rules that were carefully outlined and previously agreed upon; he always followed protocols but knew it was hopeless to argue and didn't want to make a scene. He just shook his head and rolled his eyes at both women.

Kathy was persuasive and kept moving the wheelchair toward Sophie's room to give her friend the best night of her new life and gave them both the quiet signal.

After Kathy glanced in to confirm that Sophie was asleep, she quietly wheeled her friend into the back of the large hospital room - near the door - where it was dark, should Sophie awake. Without skipping a beat, Kathy proudly handed over Sophie's chart, but all Sandra noticed was the sweetness of Austin snuggled next to his wife as they both slept after having delivered their bundle of joy. They were starting their new phase of life as a family with Sandra just feet away from them, and they didn't even know she was there. Pure elation and joy overcame her at seeing how peaceful they looked at this late hour.

As Sarah lovingly gazed at her family, she reached out to hold her friend's hand and unexpectedly got Jason's. She reached out her other hand for Kathy, and the three quietly gazed at the sleeping new parents while all holding hands. It was an amazing feeling, and each loved the historic moment for different reasons:

Kathy for reconnecting with her best friend; Sandra for seeing her granddaughter, Sophie, and Austin; Jason wasn't sure what but knew something good was stirring in his heart.

Chapter 55

Kathy wheeled her friend back into the restroom for her goodbyes and received her reminder about the severe consequences to the Stevens family if she divulged anything about the night's encounter.

"Thank you for taking such great care of my daughter," said Sarah. "If Oleg is ever caught or killed, I *will* return—without any disguises and we will party it up!"

The two hugged and said their goodbyes behind the private restroom door as Jason knocked to signal it was time to go. Kathy helped them out a back door that wasn't manned and gave Jason a reassuring pat on his back as he walked past. And before she could blink, the two of them were gone. She returned to the desk and sat with a smile on her face- what an amazing reunion she thought.

Kathy was soon interrupted as she heard two of the labor and delivery nurses chatting about the unusual visitor they saw earlier looking at the babies. Kathy snapped out of her blissful state and asked who the nurses were talking about. Nurse Della confirmed she had seen a rather awkward, middle-aged, un-friendly-looking man who was looking around the ward and had just been at the window by himself moments ago.

"Did you call security on him?" Kathy nervously asked, knowing who it could have been.

"We were about to, but he disappeared- we don't know where he went," Della responded. Kathy quickly commanded the other nurse to call security under the auspices of a potential baby abductor to get people moving quickly, grabbed her sweater, and asked Della to go outside with her to help spot him. They looked everywhere but couldn't find the strange man. By now, the hospital's security team was running all over trying to find him, but it was too late; he knew how to leave in a hurry and was gone.

Kathy had been unable to help her friend and feared the man Della had seen was the same man Nicholas had talked about, Oleg Sokotov! After reviewing the recorded footage with the security officers and seeing the strange man on the camera, Kathy immediately asked Della to accompany her to the police station to see if she could ID the man from a mug shot. Kathy had followed the trial, had conversations with Nicholas and knew the police were still looking for Oleg. Kathy felt powerless to help her friend who couldn't be reached or warned! Kathy was determined to follow up with the authorities on who the man might be, to secretly help her dear friend.

Chapter 56

As Jason drove toward the Santa Barbara airport, he noticed a car that seemed to be following them and pulled over to see if the car would continue past them or stop. The unknown car continued, passed them, but then pulled over not too far ahead and turned off its headlights.

Not good, thought Jason. Who was his tail, and what did they want at this late hour of the night?

Jason grabbed his military-issued night vision goggles from a bag under the front seat to learn more. He focused on the driver, got the license plate info, and called in an inquiry to his agency contacts. He also requested they call the local authorities to report a fake auto accident on their non-traceable phone lines, listing the area where the mystery car was pulled over as the crash site. Within minutes sirens could be heard approaching and, as anticipated, the mystery car left. When Jason received the report back on the car as being stolen, his heart sank. He knew he had a problem. He did feel the excitement that it could be Oleg and he was still catchable, but also fear that Sandra's identity and life were compromised. His first order of business was to get her back on the plane safe and sound…. ASAP.

Sandra was used to all of Jason's protocols and didn't even notice the concern on his face or the fact that they had even pulled over. Her eyes were closed with her head tilted back and mind remembering the encounter with her kids, best friend, and new grandbaby. Once more, she had been acknowledged for who she was—Kathy had called her Sarah, not Sandra! This was a big thing for her, and it gave her peace, knowing she still had a confidant who was committed to keeping her secret. Sandra was oblivious to anything outside her own world and was reveling in the joy of her visit while Jason worried for them both.

Sandra mechanically went through the routine of boarding the plane and didn't even notice Jason's extended conversation with the pilots. The happy, new grandmother was oblivious to the possible security breach that had just occurred and the need to change their flight plans. Per FBI protocol, no flight plan is ever filed until the agent on board instructs the pilots of the destination. A flight plan is never given in advance of boarding and most of the time can change even while during the route. She didn't even notice the extra call to Director Vargas, but she did pick up on Jason's change of behavior and tone of voice. She found herself hoping he wasn't mad about Kathy discovering her secret.

"Is everything okay?" she politely inquired.

"I'm just tired," he responded quickly. "It's late, and I want to get going."

She accepted his explanation and retreated back into her state of bliss.

Jason had seen the pain and sadness that Sandra had gone through from the first day they met in the elevator. He didn't want to rain on her parade. Even though today didn't go as planned, she was elated and deserved some happiness in her life, if even for a brief moment. The day had exceeded her expectations despite almost being a disaster. He could tell she was in a good mood and wanted her to enjoy that state of mind for as long as she could but had to balance in the current situation needing immediate action.

Jason also knew she would find out soon

enough of the necessary diversion away from Idaho. He decided to turn the whole thing around in his favor by convincing her of his decision to commemorate the day by flying to Florida to celebrate in the much-welcomed warmer weather. By the time they landed, and with the time zone change, it would be morning there, so it made sense to go for it and not stop in Idaho, he told himself. After all, it was the weekend!

Sandra was elated at the news and ceremoniously unbuckled her seat belt, stood up, and turned the sound system on full throttle, playing her favorite dance music from her youth compliments of the Walkman she always had with her. She was a full-fledged (young) grandparent now but started to groove like she was at a high school Sadie Hawkins dance, and awkwardly asked the man sitting across from her to stand up and dance.

Jason enjoyed seeing a happy Sandra and decided it was okay to share in the joyous mood. He put aside his concerns for the moment and stood up to dance with the happy woman. Jason managed to get a few not-so-slick dance moves going and knew he would be upstaged by her. They also managed to chat over the music, laughing at Kathy's quick thinking to keep her friend in the bathroom, celebrating the new life just born- all while dancing in the narrow aisle of the plane. It was a sight to see the two of them doing their dance moves as the plane sped toward its cruising speed and out of the reach of Oleg Sokotov.

The extra flight time was meant to cover their tracks, and Jason prayed it had worked. He wondered why he didn't listen to his instincts about the risky trip that gave Sandra away both to her friend and enemy all within the same hour. Two questions haunted him. Could Kathy keep the secret? Was the tail to the airport Oleg or one of his associates and did they recognize Sarah at the hospital or while leaving it? He would hear the answer soon enough from Director Vargas who would not be pleased with the close call. But for now, Jason might as well enjoy spending extra time with his charge. After all, he had sworn to protect her at all costs. They were headed to Florida to go where neither had been before—Miami.

Both got in some beach time and enjoyed each other's company and conversations about past lives but with the rule that anything discussed had to be fun or positive. They rented bikes and even took some impromptu salsa dance lessons during the short trip together. It appeared that Jason had some rhythm and knew how to move his dance partner around the dance floor which impressed Sandra and allowed her to be close to a man. Jason kept it light but enjoyed seeing his special friend smile for the twelve hours they had in Miami. He too enjoyed Sandra in his arms dancing and felt a special bond developing with her.

By the time they got to the airport both were exhausted and fell asleep on the plane ride back to Idaho.

Chapter 57

Oleg had been monitoring the Stevens family for a while now. He had seen Sophie's baby bump and knew she was pregnant. It would be easy to tap her phone and listen in for hints of her going into labor and the trip to the hospital to have her baby. If Dr. Stevens was still alive, the cunning criminal thought it logical that she would try to see her daughter. He didn't know if his hunch was correct, but he knew he needed to be there.

Later, when he saw the older lady getting into the dark car way too easily for someone confined to a wheelchair, he was intrigued enough to follow the car when it left. His hunch paid off. What would two older people be doing at a private airport hangar this late at night after being at a hospital? And how was it that the cops were called to where he had pulled off the road ahead of the suspicious car?

Oleg knew he was onto something and that

something had to be that Dr. Sarah Stevens was alive! He decided to call his resources for help in tracking where the late flight out of Santa Barbara was headed. He could sense his quarry drawing closer with this first real break. He just had to find and dispose of her, giving him the leeway to freely claim and run the Kozlovs' business empire without worrying about that witness emerging. Dr. Stevens's life was still worth a lot of money.

Chapter 58

As other opportunities for observing her family came and went, Sandra, realized that time had started to pick up and wasn't as painful as it once had been when she first moved to Idaho. A part of her had hoped the same for her family back in Santa Barbara, but she also hoped they had not forgotten her.

"It's time to visit the so-called happiest place on Earth," Jason said over the phone one day. "Your family's going on their annual expedition to Disneyland next week. Wanna go?"

"Heck, yeah! Is that a trick question?" Sandra quipped like an excited schoolgirl.

For many years since the kids were little, her family made a weekend of going to Disneyland. It had become a tradition to do this every first weekend in December to see all the holiday decorations and to be there when the theme park was less crowded. Going in the summer when the park was packed was verboten: too many people equaled exceptionally long lines to get on the rides.

Many a holiday photo was taken at Disneyland and sent out as the family Christmas card. Nicholas was no doubt trying to keep that tradition alive with his new granddaughter, now about two years old. Or maybe her kids insisted they all go. Either way, it would be fun to see her family with big smiles. It was a date!

Jason and the FBI agreement would not allow for a full weekend of fun, but one day with a different disguise should be fine. She had used the old lady look too many times and didn't want to be recognized that way anymore. With her short, blond hair and slimmed-down body, heavy sunglasses, and floppy hat, she could easily blend in. In fact, she could make it work looking like someone ten years younger!

Jason would still need to change up his look and decided Sandra needed two items this time around: a fake tattoo in case her arm was exposed, and a wedding ring to make it look like they were married.

"What?!" she laughed when she heard his plan and then coyly asked, "No calling me Mom or Granny anymore?"

"Not this time, dear heart," he sarcastically replied with a smile she could detect on the phone.

"So Agent Jason, if we're married, I should be asking you some questions about our life and what you do when not with me," she politely asked. "What are your hobbies? Tell me about your family."

Didn't we cover some of that in Miami and during other trips out? He wondered.

Jason had avoided talking about his past and life for important reasons of not wanting to divulge too much to a charge. Jason was caught off guard but found her playfulness welcoming and answered a few of her questions about his past relationships, parents, brother, what he did before the FBI (or at least what he was able to share,) school, and a few other tidbits.

"So Jason, tell me about what you were like in high school? What were you into—sports or what?"

"Well, actually I was a bit of a nerd. I studied a lot."

"I didn't get that studious vibe from you," she quipped. "I pictured you more of a jock wearing a letterman jacket!"

Both laughed, with Sandra jumping back in with her next round of questions, starting out with, "Any siblings or other family members like close cousins or? Besides your one brother?"

"No"

"That's it? Just, no?" she demanded. "Inquiring minds need to know for the upcoming trip - dear!"

"You do know that you are still not allowed to talk while at the park and in front of people so why all these questions, Sandra?" Jason asked trying to take back control of the conversation without deflating her excitement for the next trip out. Jason was used to asking questions, not answering them, and found it initially awkward. She had not really asked him about his past other than a few softball questions while in Miami. The agent was careful not to divulge too much but did give what he thought she should know for the upcoming visit which had nothing to do with her disguise. He knew everything about her, but she knew little about *him*, and he felt it was okay to share *some* information with her as long as he kept it brief. All in all, he found her easy to talk to at this stage of the relationship.

The one question that threw him off was, "When was the last time you visited the gun range to practice your skills?"

Jason found that question odd but admitted to her that he was long overdue. She jumped at the chance to unnerve her protector and slyly suggested he arrive early for their trip to Disneyland.

"I think it would be interesting to learn a bit about guns and how to shoot – especially since there's a shooting gallery at Disneyland" she claimed. "Maybe we can go to the local gun range so you can teach me a few things about guns before we take off?."

"OK," He sounded surprised. "We can do that."

He agreed to pick her up an hour earlier to hit the local gun range before their next flight together. Then, after playing the 20 Questions game that turned into what felt like 50 questions to Jason, the call ended with Sandra knowing a bit more about her protector and looking forward to their 'play date' at the range. She was determined to get the protective Jason to open up and be more like himself, whoever that was!

Chapter 59

The weekend arrived quicker than Sandra expected. Jason walked into her kitchen bright and early with a smile that told her he was in a good mood, too. After their protocol discussion on what, when, where, and how to fit in at Disneyland, their first order of business would be to find the Stevens family. Jason's plan was to accidentally bump into Nicholas and drop a tracking device – that looked like something out of a crackerjack box - into his back pocket, allowing them to know where the family was within the park. A second one would be dropped into one of the kids' pockets. Whoever had the best pockets for the device would be selected. Can't miss two tracking devices! It would be easy for Sandra to initially find them; she had a fairly good idea where they would be during the early part of the day.

But first, Jason made good on his promise and took Sandra to the local gun range. He didn't know that she had been practicing with her instructor nor did he know that she even had her own gun hidden in her bedroom for protection. After his thorough lecture and safety talk, Jason handed the Smith and Wesson semi-automatic revolver over. She cocked and fired it like a pro, with all shots clustered near the center of the bullseye! Jason couldn't believe his eyes, looked at the confident woman standing next to him and knew he had been hoodwinked by the fair Sandra. He laughed out loud while shaking his head in both disbelief and approval.

"Okay, Annie Oakley, you got me!" He exclaimed. "Looks like you've been a busy girl. Any other surprises for me today?"

"Nope, not today. Time to play, we're burning daylight!" she playfully stated. "Got a plane to catch – it's time to go!"

Sandra grabbed her things and headed out the door leaving Jason to put away the guns and catch up with his overly confident charge.

Both were going to have a fun day!

Chapter 60

It was just as Sandra had figured—they easily found her family at Disneyland, and the tracking devices were successfully planted. Sandra waited around the corner in Sleeping Beauty's castle and claimed upon Jason's return that she was waiting for her prince! After the devices were tested and found to be in working order, they kept their distance and observed the happy family members on their annual play date. The time was made even more delightful by watching the addition of her granddaughter to the festivities. The observers could go on *all* the same rides as the family, just not at the same time, and had to make sure to keep a good distance between them in the lines. Jason and Sandra wore dark glasses, hats, and had stashed another outfit to change their looks in the lockers by the front gate.

With her sleeves rolled up, Sandra purposely exposed her fake tattoo that Jason had carefully applied onto her arm while on the plane, just in case. Sandra enjoyed how he held her arm and applied pressure to it but worried he might have seen her goosebumps. When it was done, they both smiled at each other in admiration of the fake artwork.

It was a fun day that allowed Sandra to forget the fact that Nicholas had brought his new wife to the traditional family outing. She seemed to be friendly and interacted with the Stevens family as if they had all been together a long time. Sandra knew Nicholas would pick a nice woman to share his life with, but it was rewarding to see her family be accepting of her as well. Sandra had expected this and made peace with it, knowing her husband was once again happy and had moved on from his grieving. They all looked good together, and that brought about some peace for Sandra though she still missed Nicholas.

As the family kept on their pre-assigned path around Disneyland, Sandra kept reminding herself they needed to keep their distance. On several occasions, Jason steered her to another nearby ride in case any of her family members noticed the cute couple nearby a few too many times.

Even though she wasn't pretending to be an older woman today, she found herself grabbing Jason's arm to point something out or to guide him to the next ride. She didn't realize she was giving *him* goosebumps.

Jason was glad he could hide his eyes behind sunglasses! He had been softening up to this brave woman. He felt his heart changing and knew he couldn't do a thing about it. He looked at her differently; she wasn't just a 'job' anymore. Jason cared for this accomplished woman and the amazing heart she had for all around her. She was everything he had hoped to meet and settle down with, yet she was also his responsibility to keep safe. She had grown on him and took his heart by surprise today as she smiled and enjoyed her freedom to have fun. Heck, the woman could fire a gun and hit her target at fifty feet out!

Jason blushed at the thoughts he was having and decided to go for it by putting his arm around her. When she looked up, he quickly blurted out, "We need to keep in character!" Yet after he had said those words, he wished he hadn't.

She silently agreed. Sandra acknowledged the gesture and smiled as she turned away, wondering which side of the fence her protector was on. The question was quickly dismissed as they discussed whether to go on Splash Mountain or not. They agreed to go without the Stevens family anywhere near them. With their hats and glasses off and stowed in front of them, they agreed to cover their faces as they rocketed toward the bottom of the vertical water drop, where cameras were hidden to record the surprise splash they received at the end.

It was fun seeing her kids having a great time and being kids themselves. The tracking devices were a godsend and made their day run smoothly with no one being the wiser to their identities. The Stevens family looked happy, and her little granddaughter was just as cute as any toddler could be wearing a Tinkerbell costume.

Chapter 61

The plane trip home went by fast, with Jason wanting to deliver the best news of all at the end of the trip. He had wanted to share it at the start of their day together but decided it would be perfect to share the incredible news at the end once they got away from everyone - and wouldn't you know it? Sandra fell asleep on the plane ride home!

As they drove into her garage and parked, she jumped out so quickly he had to blurt out his gratitude while getting out of the car.

"Sandra, thank you for such a fun day and for sharing your family tradition with me," he exclaimed. "I had only been to Disneyland once before, so I had a great time. And boy, do you know how to navigate around that place!"

She smiled, and before she could say anything, Jason confidently walked over to her.

"Sandra, I have some great news to share with you," he continued.

"The Kozlov brothers were murdered in

prison about a week ago. They are gone! I wanted to tell you in person – not over the phone – I had to see your reaction – man this was really hard to hold in all day!"

"What… oh my gosh, oh my God… it's almost done!!!" Sandra exclaimed with happiness at the realization that her journey in witness protection was now partly done.

She was overjoyed and filled with so much hope that she ran into Jason's arms and hugged him hard, whispering over and over, "Thank you, thank you, thank you! I don't want to know the details, just that they're gone!"

She kept holding onto him for fear that if she let go, the news wouldn't be true.

The Kozlov brothers, their family holdings, and businesses were on their way out. Oleg had not stepped up to run the businesses for fear of being caught, so competitors violently took over the illegal activities and interests, which sent remaining members of the Kozlov family out of the country to avoid more bloodshed. It was rumored that these same people had caused the deaths of the Kozlov brothers to keep them or their associates from interfering with their take-over.

Since Oleg was still at large, he continued to pose a real threat- especially if he aspired to reclaim the Kozlovs' empire on his own. Jason knew Oleg was out there somewhere and seemed to have surmised that Dr. Stevens was still alive and a threat to his aspirations—and his survival. It was just a matter of time before he and/or his network of thugs found her. Jason knew this and held her in his arms a bit longer than he should have. As she pulled back from their embrace, she looked up and quickly kissed his cheek goodbye.

"Thank you again for the incredible day," she said, then walked into her house and locked the door behind her as instructed to do so many times before.

Jason was surprised by her kiss but loved it, wishing she hadn't disappeared into the house so quickly. His heart was hooked and officially lost to her!

She felt her flushed cheeks and wondered about Jason's feelings toward her. Was he finally warming up his once frozen and all-business facade? She couldn't think about that now. The Kozlov brothers were dead and gone. It took five years for it to happen, but it finally happened! She was now a bit closer to her freedom. If only the authorities could find Oleg, preferably dead, she would be totally free to leave Idaho and rejoin her old life in Santa Barbara.

What a rush of excitement it gave her just thinking about it! She was giddy and didn't know if part of her giddiness was a result of their day at Disneyland, the man who had just held her, or the news he had just delivered. It had been five long years without male companionship, and she knew that ache all too well. The real rush was from Jason. What a day!

Two bad guys down, one to go!

Chapter 62

Sandra was on a high, so she decided to make pumpkin bread with chocolate chips in it, Harold and Martha's favorite treat during the holidays. She wasn't a good cook but wanted to take something over to her kindly neighbors, who had all but adopted her as the daughter they wished they had. Martha had a cold, which left Harold to be the chief cook and bottle washer – which was not his thing.

As she dropped off her goodwill gesture, Harold noticed the extra kick in her step.

"Have you been drinking?" he teased. "I can always tell when Martha's had a bit of something when she's as happy as you seem to be!"

Sandra laughed at her neighbor's humor.

"Oh, I just received some good news the other day, so I'm in a really good mood!"

Harold laughed with her but couldn't resist asking, "Is there a new man in your life?"

Sandra stopped and had to think about that.

"I'm not sure!" she said thoughtfully. "But I

have this feeling that life is getting better, so I made this bread for you."

He smiled and gave her the paternal 'thank you' hug she so appreciated.

"Promise to come over for some holiday cheer after Martha's feeling better?"

"I promise!" she responded.

It was hard seeing all the young neighbor kids getting excited about Christmas and wishing she could be a part of the festivities. Her neighbors were now all dialed in to include Sandra in their parties when they could, but to them, she wasn't married and didn't have kids, which meant zero invites to those child-centric types of celebrations. The adults-only events were few and far between and awkward for her as a single woman, but she loved attending whatever invite she got. She had to remind herself that she was still in hiding, but by all recent accounts, her social situation was progressing.

Sandra kept her workouts going, loved her self-defense classes, and wished she could share the news of earning her black belt with someone, but didn't. Her sensei was great to work out with, especially when he threw real-life situations her way on the mat. Little did he know the background of his star pupil and why she was so committed to learning her new craft. At most lessons, Sandra pictured the ugly Oleg coming after her which gave her the intensity to focus with her moves.

Sandra had been the most resolved and serious student Sensei Roberge had had in years. But he'd been around the block a few times teaching those who had been harmed in their past, so he understood his students' motivations to learn how to protect themselves. Her determination to finish her black belt and to then ask for more was unusual. He enjoyed her enthusiasm and zest for more and dished out what he could to push her. The sensei knew that whatever Sandra's past, she was now prepared for a more confident future.

It had now been years since she had faked her death, but not a day had gone by where her hope had dwindled about receiving the news of Oleg's demise. Her motto? Take one day at a time. She vowed to make every day count so that one day she would be able to reemerge and reconnect. Sandra lived for this and prayed every day, hoping God would grant her the most precious request she had ever asked of the

Almighty. Her faith had sustained her during her exile, but for how much longer?

One day at a time, she thought. *One day at a time.*

Little did Sandra know that Oleg was now looking for her in Idaho, although Jason was beginning to suspect it. Oleg had obtained the flight plan information logged in at the Santa Barbara Airport by hacking into their computer system. He saw the multiple flights on some of the days he monitored the family and correctly deducted by the family's actions that they didn't know about her existence. Oleg was getting closer to finding his quarry but had decided to start monitoring the family a bit more for clues. He had enlisted the help of a new thug to listen in on the family's phone calls. One call interested him enough to head back to Santa Barbara to investigate it himself.

Chapter 63

Jason and Sandra had now been on ten visits/adventures together and had become good friends, with a special interest in one another developing. She listened to his instructions each time and, without much exception successfully navigated their way to observe her family without being noticed.

The incident at the hospital with Dr. Kathy had been the only breach of her identity, but Sandra felt confident that Kathy would keep her secret and would not do anything to jeopardize her dearest friend's safety. There were a few times when Max almost gave her away, so she had learned to douse herself with perfume to hide her scent and knew not to speak - especially when Max was around. Sandra had learned many tricks of the trade to blend in and not be noticed. She could confidently help Agent Jason plan the trips and even caught him a few times missing an important detail to their day ahead. She jokingly mocked him now and then as they worked through their checklist of rules, teasing him on his thoroughness that had kept them both safe and alive.

Jason expected that Oleg would eventually make his move and when he did, Jason wanted to be there. He thought he had covered all the bases for that day's outing but had no idea how to plan for matters of the heart. Today was going to be special for Sandra.

Jason arrived at her home as a complete surprise, walking in the back door unannounced and scaring her! She screamed at the sight of someone unexpected in her kitchen.

"I'm so sorry!" he apologized. "But remember—you've got to keep your doors locked even when you're at home. Now, I've got a surprise for you! We're going to see your son!"

"What?!" she squealed with delight.

"That's all I can tell you," he teased, "other than we're headed to the beach, so dress accordingly.

Sandra had been rocking out to her stereo while doing her dishes, so Jason took over the kitchen duties and shooed her upstairs to get ready.

She immediately ran back down and asked, "What should my disguise be this time?"

"Nothing. No disguise!" he said, much to

Sandra's surprise. He was sure she wouldn't be seen in the remote area where they were headed.

"It should be around the high 70's. A summer dress should do, along with your big sun hat and glasses," Jason advised.

Boy, he sure knows every piece of clothing I have, thought Sandra. *Well, just as long as he didn't buy them!* She chuckled. Not many guys could instruct a woman on what she should wear with his level of confidence!

Sandra showered in record time, grabbed her beach stuff and the other items Jason suggested, and bounded down the stairs with gleeful anticipation, wondering what he had up his sleeve for today. All their visits were special, so she believed this one would be no different and was excited to go and find out.

The flight to Santa Barbara was like all the others, only this time, the car waiting for them was clearly not the standard-issue van but a convertible! Sandra loved the coastal drive north along the 101 highway and made sure the top was down to allow her medium-short, blond hair to get messed up by the cool ocean breezes. She missed the West Coast beaches, and Jason knew it.

Chapter 64

The drive up the Santa Barbara coast was heaven for Sandra as she took in the direct sunlight wearing large, Jackie O-type sunglasses. The weather couldn't have been more perfect had she ordered it up herself. Jason didn't drive at his normal crazy pace and seemed to be enjoying the weather, too. Yet he was still all 'eagle eyes,' looking around for something to be worried about as they turned off the highway and pulled into an informal parking area, shared by the train tracks that overlooked the ocean and beach below. To reach the beach, one had to climb down a somewhat steep hill to find the secluded local surf spot.

As they exited the car to enjoy the view, Sandra immediately recognized where they were. And the old Jeep parked nearby? It was Jackson's! As she started to walk toward the cliff edge past his top-open Jeep, Max jumped up from his comfortable nap position and started to whimper in recognition of his long-lost friend! Sandra looked around and, with no one to see her, lavished her favorite dog with the long-overdue affection he so deserved. Max was much older now, close to 15, which was why Jackson had left him in the Jeep with his freshwater bowl and snack nearby. Jackson always made sure Max got out and about, and today was no exception. He made sure his canine buddy was safely tethered and had a cushy pad to sit on while he surfed below.

"Oh, Maxy boy…. I'm so glad to see you – oh how I've missed you and our time together at the office and hospital…. you're such a good boy Maxy!"

Max happily whined and licked his long-lost friend's arm, showing his never-ending affection for her. While the two were catching up, Jason tapped her arm and gave her his binoculars.

"Take a look at Jackson catching the next wave," he suggested.

Jackson had been surfing since he was a little tike and loved the ocean and the peace it gave him. His mom stood up on the hill, safely out of sight to those below, and watched her son and his friend surf wave after wave – and in between - lavished Max with attention. She was so happy to see her old friend still alive and recognizing her.

While Sandra watched, Jackson saw his chance to catch one of the bigger waves forming and was set to stand on his board for what looked like the best wave of the day when he got tossed off which in turn snapped his safety leash off. The joy she'd felt watching her son surf turned to concern as his board shot up out of the violent wave without him on it. She gasped at the sight of her son getting slammed hard by the relentless waves. To make matters worse, he didn't immediately surface.

Alarmed, Sandra started running for the cliff to make her way down when Jason ran after her to pull her back. He was holding her tight as she faced forward, looking for any sign that Jackson would surface and be okay.

"He's a good athlete," Jason calmly whispered into her ear. "He knows what he's doing. He'll surface!"

Jason could feel her heart beating wildly as his arms crossed her chest to hold her back much like how he did when they jumped out of the plane with her strapped to him.

Sandra's maternal instincts were on high alert;

she wanted to run down that cliff and into the water to make sure her son was safe. It was a strong dual instinct of being both a mother and doctor that kept her squirming to break away from Jason. It appeared that Jackson's surf buddy was also concerned and had paddled to the dunking site to look for him when, out of nowhere, Jackson punched through the water and surfaced while gasping for air! He and his buddy decided to take a break and swam in together when Sandra noticed that the buddy was not a guy but a girl!

In fact, as Jackson helped her out of the water and carried her board back to their beach towels, it seemed she was more than just any girl—they were quite cozy with each other!

Jackson had once told his mom that he hoped the girl of his dreams would enjoy surfing as much as he did. And there he was, at the beach with some young lady who was clearly more than his buddy. How sweet it was to see her son so happy. And then Sandra realized that Jason was still holding her!

Chapter 65

There they were, Sandra and Jason, standing near the cliff above the beach, his arms across the front of her body, holding her against him. She was immediately flush with a warmth that enveloped her body like she had not experienced in years. His breathing was slow and steady, and he felt every move her body made and every breath she took as he held her tightly against him. Both knew they had fires going for each other, and as she turned around to face him, his left hand shifted to slide down her back to bring her in close. They looked into each other's eyes as if asking for permission to dive into each other's soul and, in unison, embraced each other in a kiss that would send angels hiding! They held onto each other for what seemed like an eternity as they drank in their long-overdue feelings and refused to let go of their embrace.

Jason could barely talk but surfaced from the long kiss just long enough to mutter, "I've wanted to do that to you for years!" before diving back into the passionate lip lock with her.

Below, as they exchanged their affection-filled words, Jackson's girlfriend looked up and spotted the new lovebirds on the cliffs above and told Jackson to check them out as she snuggled up against him on their towels.

"Aw, isn't it wonderful to see those two people so happy?" she asked. "I wonder if they're in love as much as we are, Jackson?"

Jackson considered this comment as great timing for what he had planned. He reached under the beach towel and dug for the buried treasure he had carefully hidden from her.

"What are you doing?" she asked, perplexed but smiling.

Jackson found his treasure, stood up, gently grabbed her arm to help her up, too, and then went down on one knee to pop the most important question to his future bride.

"Kristin – I have a special ring to put on your finger and a question to ask, how about spending the rest of our lives together?" He said with a big grin and sand in his hair.

Without hesitation, she screamed her answer

so loudly and with such delight that it was heard up the cliff above, breaking the embrace Sandra and Jason were in.

It was an amazing sight for Sandra to gaze down and see her son on one knee with what looked like a ring box being opened before her very eyes. The two young adults immediately embraced and proceeded to do what Sandra and Jason had just been doing! Sandra gasped in amazement at what she had just witnessed—her son proposing to her future daughter-in-law! And how did Jason know this was going to happen? How did he get the timing so perfect?

As she quizzically looked into his eyes, all Jason could do was smile and admire the woman he'd had a crush on for years. He had wanted this moment for what felt like an eternity and wasn't quite ready to let her go, sliding his arm back around her waist to bring her in for another kiss and a serious embrace that would surely spike each other's blood pressure.

Sandra's adrenaline was in full gear as she embraced her permissible love. She thanked him profusely for the incredible observation from the safe distance. As she did so, the newly engaged couple below was digging up what looked like a bottle of Champagne to celebrate. The parallels were almost too much for Sandra to think about; her soul was on fire for Jason and his for her.

The two of them needed to escape before being discovered. In one amazing move, Jason picked up her hat, which had blown off during her attempted sprint for the beach, surveyed the perimeter, swooped up Sandra into his arms, and deposited her into the passenger side of the rental car. Yet she couldn't leave without saying goodbye to Max who had been whining and watching her every move, so got out to lavish him one last time with her trademark Max Rubdown. After a final glance around the beach, her son, and amazing coastal scenery, Sandra kissed Max goodbye and jumped back into the convertible. The two quickly drove off, leaving a bit of dust in their wake like two teenagers heading for Lover's Lane for the first time.

Jackson had seen the woman on the cliff above approach Max and give his dog what looked like his mother's famous Max Rubdown and how favorably Max had reacted to it before the couple sped off. He wondered how a total stranger could know that move.

As he processed what he had seen, his thoughts were interrupted by his newly minted fiancée's hand reaching for his to gently remind him of their special moment. Jackson proudly smiled at his future bride-to-be, hugged her tightly, and quickly forgot what puzzled him. He couldn't wait to share the good news of the impending nuptials and did so with anyone they encountered, including the stranger sitting alone in a beach chair reading his book.

"We're engaged!" Jackson gleefully shouted as the two love birds danced around in the sand.

The stranger managed a quirky nod and then left, heading up the hill to see where the couple at the top of the cliff had gone. Oleg had seen the two above and felt his patience was about to pay off. He called his contact to stand by to see if his hunch could be confirmed in Boise. The orders were to follow them and report back where they went. Oleg was closing in.

Chapter 66

As Jason sped off toward the airport, all he could think about was holding Sandra and devouring every inch of her. He drove as fast as he could, steering with one hand while caressing her with the other. The two couldn't keep their hands off each other and almost forgot their security protocols as they approached the airport and stopped just short of being seen by the crew. Jason nervously went through his security routine and, when all was clear, the doors secure, extra people out of the hangar, and cockpit windows covered, he drove the convertible to its assigned position, with Sandra hiding in the back seat with a beach towel over her head, ready to board.

After Jason got her on board and signaled the flight crew, they were ready to take off. He was immediately drawn to Sandra and grabbed her for a long and passionate embrace that didn't include seat belts! The two had a lot of catching up to do to release the bottled-up attraction they had shared but had been afraid to explore.

The flight went quickly as they sat together holding hands, wondering what would come next. By the end of the flight, both had been near their breaking point and could have used the hidden oxygen masks above them.

By the time Jason drove into her garage and closed the door, that was all she wrote. They ran into the house and up the stairs to get lost in whatever they wanted to do to each other. They were together and alone at last.

Chapter 67

As the sun peaked over the eastern horizon, neither Jason nor Sandra moved from her bed. Both were exhausted from all that had transpired the night before, which took every ounce of energy they had during their emotional and physical time together. The two slept in late and were amused when they finally started to stir.

Sandra blushed while recounting their evening. But it didn't matter—they were in love and loved what it did to their demeanors. Both were ravishingly hungry and needed fuel for their day if Round Two was to start. There wasn't much in the kitchen.

"Me go forage for food at grocery store?" Jason grunted, cave-man style.

Sandra needed some time to shower and get ready for a blissful day together so was relieved her lover offered to bring back some brunch. She grabbed her man and kissed him goodbye before he could pass through the front door.

Jason's head was clearly not on straight as he

tripped down the porch stairs on his way out, forgetting that the car was parked in the garage and not out front. Sandra was equally distracted and bumped her head on the screen door as she turned to re-enter the house. Both were messed up in love, to the amusement of Harold next door, who saw the whole comedic scene unfold from his front porch and just shook his head in disbelief.

The day was long, and both enjoyed the extra mood-inspiring music Sandra had on her stereo. The two of them had been missing the physical touch of a loved one, but that yearning was being satisfied now. The barriers had been dropped, and they were quite comfortable with each other as if they had been together for years.

But Jason would eventually have to leave. He had asked the flight crew to stay over and had no idea why or when he would be returning the jet back to its home base. He was in breach of the rules by using the government's jet for personal time. Staying over with Sandra was also clearly a violation of agency rules. He would have to explain his actions to Director Vargas and hope there were no repercussions.

As their time together ended, Sandra begged him for details.

"When can we see each other again?" she asked.

More importantly, she wondered how this unique relationship would work out given the geographical distances and his job. She could not wait another six months before seeing him again.

Jason returned to the threshold and slipped his arm around her waist and once again brought her up against him.

"I will return to your side, front side, and backside as fast as I can," he reassured her, "even if it means driving all night to spend a day together from wherever I am!"

This made her smile, which caused him to once again dive in to hold and kiss her for as long as she would allow before making his proper exit through the garage door.

Sandra couldn't remember if she had asked where he lived or not, and if she had, she couldn't remember what his response had been. She did remember his gorgeous blue eyes and the feel of his body

touching hers and how good it all felt. She would remember all these thoughts and emotions until they
were together again. They would see her through those
empty moments each day when she wasn't thinking
about reuniting with her family. What a wonderful distraction he had become to her quiet life!

Snap out of it! She thought, but then dismissed
that in favor of enjoying the long-awaited bliss she felt
she deserved. She would allow this glow to fill her for
however long it would last.

Chapter 68

Sandra was on Cloud Nine and smiled as she did the dishes, attempting to put her home back in order after the impromptu brunch. She loved hearing her favorite music blaring over the sound of the soap and water. She was in the best mood she had been in for years, having seen her son the day before and her subsequent commitment to Jason. She was happy and giddy and didn't mind the work before her.

Her mind was playing back the events of the night before when she heard what she thought was the sound of breaking glass at her back door. She froze and wondered if a bird had flown into her window or if maybe Jason had come back. Either way, she stopped what she was doing and promptly stepped back from the sink as fear gripped her. It *was* glass breaking—she was sure of it, and her heart skipped a beat at the thought of an intruder in her house.

With an immediate dose of adrenaline pulsating through her veins, Sandra quickly ducked behind the island in her kitchen and tried to listen for footsteps or anything that would give her reason to chalk up her concern as overblown, but it was hard to hear over the music blaring so loudly. As she crouched behind the kitchen island, she looked around and immediately saw the reflection in the glass oven door of a much shorter man than Jason cautiously walking through her house, holding in front of him what looked like a gun!

It was clear—he was looking for her and, by the looks of the gun, wanted to kill her. As she silently gasped, Sandra was now thankful the music was on to hide the sound of her movements as she negotiated her way around the kitchen island in the hope of making a dash for the stairs. She needed to get to her bedroom where her gun was safely stored and ready.

As Oleg walked around, he didn't notice her reflection in the oven. But after seeing the soap bubbles in the kitchen sink, he knew she must be around somewhere close by. As he was looking at the sink, Sandra made her move and ran upstairs, hoping the creaky floorboards wouldn't give her away. Yet it almost didn't matter, as the intruder would eventually make his way up there, and she knew she had a limited amount of time to be ready.

For years Sandra had been training for the day she might have to defend herself. Today was the day, whether she was ready or not. She had been to the gun range and was confident in her ability to shoot her gun, but it's a lot different shooting at a piece of paper fifty feet away than it is shooting a live human being trying to shoot you back. Intellectually she knew this to be true, but now she was faced with a life-or-death situation that could happen within seconds. She wasn't sure of herself under those conditions.

Sandra had also acquired her black belt in karate. Kenpo was the discipline she had studied, but how could she fight off a man with a gun who was twenty feet away and could shoot her before she reached him? Kenpo would only be effective if he was close to her, but his gun meant she wouldn't be able to defend herself that way. Her gun would have to defend her.

She prayed the intruder would go away if he thought someone was home, so she made some noise as she carefully closed and locked her bedroom door then moved to retrieve her gun hidden in a purse stashed at the top of her closet. Sandra moved to the threshold of her bathroom door, which would be out of his line of sight, and waited.

Oleg figured Dr. Stevens had to be upstairs and turned to head up there when the back door flew open, exposing an elderly man holding a rifle. Oleg quickly reeled around and shot the man, winging him in the arm. Poor Harold fell back and was knocked out when his head hit the floor as his rifle fired. Oleg knew he should backtrack to shoot the old man again, but time was of the essence. Even if his intended target was upstairs, she would have heard the gunshot and might be hiding or fleeing. Worse yet, the neighbors could have heard the shot and called the police if she hadn't already, so Oleg purposely started his way upstairs to quickly finish the job and leave.

Upon hearing the gunshot, Sandra knew she was in trouble.

Chapter 69

"Sarrrrrah Stevvvvvens, we need to talk," she heard the man creepily call out to her as he climbed the stairs toward her.

"Where are you, Sarah? It's okay. I won't hurt you. I just need to talk to you." She could confirm his whereabouts by hearing the creaky noises made by the stairs he stepped on.

The man climbing the stairs had to be Oleg Sokotov, and he wasn't there to talk. He knew her real name – he called out her real name! Her heart all but jumped out of her chest as she tried to control her fear. As Oleg reached the top of the stairs, the locked bedroom door was no match for his quick shot at the handle. With one swift kick, Oleg had the door open and was peering into the bedroom to locate his target, still calling out to her to get a response that would help confirm her whereabouts for his bullets.

Sandra had closed and locked her bathroom door and squatted down behind the small wall that created a separate vanity space from the bathroom sink.

She used the wall to help steady her gun at the door should Oleg get through it. She tried to play out her options, but adrenaline and fear gripped her thought process. All she could think to do was aim her gun at the door and wait for fate to play out its hand.

As she heard Oleg open her closet door looking for her, Sandra heard the music go silent downstairs and could now hear the floorboards creak again as Oleg walked toward her bathroom door. This is it! she thought. Something was going to happen. She wanted the upper hand and she wanted to live. She was prepared to shoot whoever stepped through her bathroom door! She had the angle and would have the element of surprise on her side. She had played out this possible scene in her head a thousand times over the years and would now trust her instincts and skills. As the floorboards beneath Oleg's feet gave away his position, Sandra stood up and fired her gun using every shot the magazine had creating holes all over the thin bathroom walls that allowed her bullets to get through to their intended target.

As she fired, she heard a round of gunfire going off outside, with one of the bullets piercing the bathroom wall and hitting the shower tiles. No one had gotten through the locked bathroom door, but she heard yelling, more gunshots, and then silence.

Finally, she heard the heavenly sound of Jason shouting, "Sandra - It's okay, Sandra. Where are you?"

How did Jason know Oleg had come in? Sandra tried to stop shaking, but until she was safe in his arms, her body wouldn't cooperate, and violently gave up the brunch.

Chapter 70

"I'm coming in!" Jason yelled, knowing that Sandra might have her gun out.

He rushed in to see her heaving and grabbed a towel for her to clean up.

"Grab your medical bag or first aid kit—whatever you have!" he shouted. "My dad's been shot - hurry!"

Sandra did have a medical kit of sorts, but this one was in a paper bag and put together in case someone on her street needed something quick. She wasn't sure of Jason's orders but steadied herself, grabbed the paper bag, and ran downstairs to find her favorite neighbor, Harold, passed out in a pool of blood. She cried out at the sight but went to work to find the source of the wound.

"Call 911," she said as calmly as she could, not knowing Jason had already done so. Then she worked to locate the source of the wound. His *dad?* she wondered.

"Did you call Harold your dad?" Sandra asked

before changing gears to pronounce that Harold's arm was the only place hit as she completed her quick exam. "He'll be okay, but he's lost a lot of blood. He probably hit his head when he fell backward from the shot. We need to get him to the hospital."

"Paramedics are on their way," Jason confirmed, "along with the police."

Jason decided to gingerly let the cat out of the bag, not sure what Sandra's reaction would be.

"Harold and Martha are my parents," he explained. "I wanted to tell you sooner, but I thought it better to keep that tidbit to the side. You had enough to deal with! My dad is a retired Marine, so I'm not sure how his buddies will treat him when they hear how he was shot and didn't get the bad guy!"

As he was finishing his sentence, the sirens were heard headed their way.

I'll be right back – gotta check on my mom!" Jason said and then ran next door before Sandra could react to anything that was happening around her.

As Harold came to and was being taken care of by the paramedics, he was relieved to see his sweet neighbor and asked what had happened. He divulged that he was the one who had called his son to return.

"Jason told me that if anything ever happened to you, I would cease to exist!" he said with a smile. After you two finished bumping your heads on your front porch and Jason left, I noticed a car parked under a tree two houses down – it was there yesterday and this morning, so I kept an eye on it. A man got out and walked over... I was observing him from the living room where he couldn't see me, but I could see him. When he opened your backyard gate next to mine– I got a good look at him and called Jason who had just left you. I got my gun and went after him."

Harold had provided just the right amount of delay to Oleg's moves to give his son the chance to return and confront Oleg. Though, Harold had wanted a piece of Oleg himself and had intended to stop him.

All Sandra could do was smile and shake her head in pleasant disbelief.

"I think you've done an incredible job of raising your son!" she stated coyly. "I would love to spill the beans about our adventures after you get home from the hospital. But for now, you need to get looked over and stitched up – Doctors orders!"

Harold winked at Sandra and gave her hand a loving squeeze with his good hand. He frowned at the thought of going to the hospital and getting poked and prodded by the hospital staff but started smiling again once Martha was at his side.

The coroner arrived at the scene while Sandra looked for Jason amongst the many neighbors now present to see what had happened and found him talking on his satellite phone to, she figured, Director Vargas. The director would need to know all the details of what had just happened. She thought Jason would want to know how his dad was doing and stood next to him… holding his hand while he said 'hi' to his old neighbors that hadn't seen him in years.

Then it hit her—she was *free*! The separation from her family could now be over! It was all over!!!!

Chapter 71

It had been a few days since Oleg had been killed in her home, but it didn't matter anymore. Over the years, Sandra had prayed for the day she would be free – the day her life in secret exile would end. The flame of that hope had never been extinguished and now her prayers were answered. Harold was released from the hospital after a quick overnight observation by the prodders and claimed it was time to celebrate over dinner. He and Martha invited their other son Jimmy and his family to join them as well.

As the door opened to greet Jimmy and his family, Jason brought his lover over and, while holding hands, introduced Dr. Sarah Stevens, known to many as just Sarah, to his family. Sarah's eyes teared up at the sound of her name. Her true and real name was Sarah, and she had longed for the day it could be said without fear of harm. She would later have Jason say it over and over in her ear behind closed doors.

Sarah loved meeting his family, and all sat around the table getting to know the woman Jason had been holding hands with non-stop while sitting tall and proud in his chair. None of the Bennett family had ever seen him so happy, not even with his ex when all was good before the divorce. And just like that, it was apparent that Jason's last name was Bennett and how clever was he to hide that fact from her. Glancing from the dining room table, Sarah could see the many photos of Jason that were once hidden, now proudly displayed on the walls. Martha made sure they were all back up for the happy occasion.

Other neighbors stopped by for dessert, and all was celebratory, though most had no idea of what had really happened or the true story behind their neighbor known only to them as Sandra. They just thought an intruder happened to enter Sandra's home.

Sarah particularly enjoyed the stories she heard from the older neighbors about Jason when he was a younger man. It was all good to her as she wanted to hear more of these stories that connected Jason's past to these people and to the neighborhood. He had hidden those truths so adeptly from her. She now understood why he drove into the garage to not be seen by the neighbors and why Harold and Martha didn't have any photos of their 'other' son. So many puzzle pieces started to come together and make sense – she wondered how she missed all those details and clues.

As the evening was concluding, Jason's phone went off. After seeing who the caller was, he decided it was important enough to take it amid the sea of people but stepped outside so no one could hear the conversation. It was a quick one and confirmed what he had hoped.

Jason walked over to Sarah and gave her a big hug, which she just couldn't get enough of these days.

"Tomorrow," he whispered in her ear, "I'm taking you home Sarah!"

Chapter 72

Sarah could hardly sleep and stayed awake wondering what she would say to her family. She had dreamed of this moment for years and had played out all the possible scenes. But she was now blank for words and thoughts as just feelings flooded her at the realization of what would happen. She knew she would have to be careful about presenting herself and wondered if Director Vargas was going to help her out in some way. Would he talk to her family first? Just how does one rise from the dead to be reintroduced to their family?

To the best of Jason's knowledge, no one had emerged seven years after entering the Witness Protection Program the way Sarah was about to. It was decided that only her immediate family -which included Nicholas and his wife - would be present to meet with her, and then, from there everyone would take it one day at a time to see what worked best for all involved.

As the morning sun rose, Sarah was already up and getting ready for what would be one of the happiest days of her life. After a few good-luck hugs and kisses from Martha and Harold, Jason opened the car door for his Sarah, and off they went toward their memorable and historic day.

Jason was concerned about Sarah seeing Nicholas, but those thoughts were quickly dismissed when upon exiting the car, Sarah initiated a very passionate kiss and hug before boarding the plane.

As their last FBI flight together landed at Santa Barbara's airport, and the plane taxied to the hangar, Sarah couldn't resist the temptation to break away from the previous strict protocols and knocked on the cockpit door. As it opened, and to the amazement of the pilots, she asked them to come out so she could give each one a big hug and smooch on the cheek to thank them for keeping her safe these last seven years. To Jason's amusement, she didn't know that the pilots had been changed a few times during those years, but it wouldn't have mattered to her if they did; she was compelled to thank them.

Now in her old stomping grounds in Santa Barbara, Sarah was anxious about how she would be reunited with her family. But Jason had something else in mind. Instead of turning south on the freeway, he drove north to the same beach area that they had been at the week before where they had witnessed her son's engagement. But more importantly to Jason, this was where he and Sarah had first kissed and exposed their true feelings for one another.

The two got out of the car and walked to the edge of the small cliff that showcased an incredible view up and down the coastline. Sarah was not sure why they were at this beach again and momentarily thought that this was where her family might be as she scanned the area for signs of their presence. Jason smiled and took in a deep breath of the beautiful day as he reached for her hands, dropped down on one knee, and professed his love for her and the need to marry her as soon as possible. Sarah screamed with a delight that could be heard over the waves and down the beach! Once again, the two did what they did best—getting lost in each other's arms and making out like a pair of hormone-driven teenagers!

This time it was Sarah who broke away first.

"Yes, Jason, *yes*! I will marry you and love you forever!" she said through tears of joy. "If we can survive the last few years together, we can survive anything together!"

"That's all I wanted to hear. I'm head over heels for you! I'm yours forever, even if you can't cook for beans!" he quipped to break up the seriousness of the moment and to see her big smile.

"And… I love your granny look," he continued. "It's sexy!" Jason was batting a thousand for her continuous, non-stop smiles!

There was no question about it—they were passionate about each other. But Sarah needed to march on to the finish line, eager at continuing the journey toward seeing her family, and would now do so triumphantly with Jason by her side.

Chapter 73

The Stevens family was assembled at the empty church where they all had worshiped for many years. None of them knew what was happening or why they were called there. The FBI had contacted each of them the day before and requested they appear at this church on this date and time.

None of them had heard anything about the missing Oleg in years, only that he was still at large, and they were concerned about what they would learn today. It unnerved them to think about him and what he did to their matriarch. The family chatter was nervous, with each wondering if something wrong had happened. Finally, Director Vargas walked in with several agents and called the family to huddle up for a chat. Susan started to tear up as she feared the worst, and not even Max could calm her nerves.

"What's wrong now?" she blurted out. "Why are you here and why are we... what happened?"

As the director started to talk and calm the family's fears, Sarah and Jason arrived outside the church and prepared to walk in. As the director talked to the bewildered family, the agents who had watched over the Stevens for years all walked in and lined up at the back wall of the church with smirks on their faces – including her attorney Mr. Benowitz. The family turned around and became confused and unnerved at the sight of the very agents they knew seven years ago lining up near the back door. Even Mrs. Mueller was there, and a flood of unsettling memories caused the family to fear their fate and question what was going on. Why were the agents all back? All were concerned and caused Susan to cry.

Outside, Jason was opening the car door for his fiancée and had planned on walking her in when she quickly popped out, caressed his face in her hands, planted a big, lipstick-stained kiss on his cheek, then turned and ran for the church door. She just couldn't stand it any longer and bolted into the church, stopping to stand silently, looking at her kids, her granddaughter, Nicholas, and his wife. They were all there, squinting to see who had walked in.

The west-facing church door was still open when Jason walked in, sunlight pouring in and casting a back-lit shadow on Sarah. Her family couldn't tell who she was until the door closed and Max started to whimper. He trotted to his old friend's side, moaning his approval. Sarah knelt to love her old dog and sweetly talked to Max for all to hear.

Recognizing the once well-known voice, it started to sink in that she might be their Sarah! As Max confirmed her identity by his whining vocals, the others stared in wonder and disbelief that the different-looking woman before them was their loved one and not some angel who just flew in the door. They cautiously ran towards her with tears and in utter shock – crying out to her.

As the family hugged and cried together, the director spoke up and shared a brief version of what she had been through. Within seconds, the disbelief turned to a realization which caused a pure emotional release by all in the room as the family reunited and touched their Sarah for confirmation that she was real.

Somewhere amid that giant family hug was a determined woman who had gone the distance to save her family at the cost of seven years of her life. Doing what she thought was the right thing to do – she did not give up - and had always hoped for this day to arrive and the ordeal to be over.

Nicholas stood back and allowed their kids to circle their mom and tried to process what was happening as he too was in utter shock at the sight of the woman he had once mourned coming back to life.

The agents present at this reunion found it hard not to tear up, for they, too, had been witnesses to the family's ordeal as they continued their protection around the clock that first year. They had seen them mourn their mom and Nicholas his wife. Only the director and Jason knew that Sarah was alive and hiding in Idaho. Upon hearing of the pending reunion, all agents that were involved with the family wanted to witness her return and were moved to hear of her sacrifice.

Dr. Sarah Steven's Sacrificial Deal became infamous within that small circle of agents and those involved with the case. But from that day on it was kept a secret to continue the anonymity.

Chapter 74

The stunned family talked and showered their beloved matriarch with questions, but it was Jackson who finally asked about the man who was standing close behind his mom, as he seemed different from the other agents in the room. Sarah smiled and reached for Jason's hand.

"Everyone, I'd like to introduce you to Agent Jason Bennett," she began. "He is the man who saved my life, in more ways than one! He is also now my fiancée!"

As her surprised children introduced themselves, Sarah walked over to Nicholas, who was clearly still in shock, gave him a kiss on the cheek, and then hugged his wife who was really surprised but appreciative of the accepting gesture. There were many things that Sarah had wanted to say to Nicholas, but all he really needed to know was that she was supportive of his choice to remarry and hopeful that they could remain long-term friends.

Nicolas was speechless and stunned at Sarah's

return and new look. But he managed to clear his throat enough to congratulate Jason on their recent decision to marry and shook his hand hard to show admiration and thanks for what he did for his long-lost wife.

Susan kept hugging her mom as if to see if she was real.

"Sweet Susan, you need to catch me up on your choice of schools," Sarah said gently. "UCSB. I was surprised."

Susan just smiled. "It's a long story, but I'll tell you all about it real soon, Mom! It's a good one!"

Sophie proudly introduced her mother to her grandchild, now almost a five-year-old.

"My, my, Sarah – you are becoming such a big girl!" called her grandmother as she reached to give her namesake a hug. The family was befuddled. How did she know her granddaughter's name?

"Mom?" Sophie asked, looking squarely at her mother. "Were you somehow there at the hospital when my Sarah was born?"

The proud grandmother smiled and told Sophie about her brief visit that night and the experience of seeing her daughter and Austin resting before the baby's next feeding.

"I thought you were there!" Sophia exclaimed. "But then I figured it was all just a dream!"

Jackson stepped forward and blurted out, "Mom, I'd like to introduce you to *my* fiancée! Her name is Kristen, and we just got engaged!"

"Yes, I know, Jackson," she said with a smile. "At the beach where you surf, yes?"

"Mom, was that you at the top of the knoll by my Jeep, petting Max?"

"Yes, honey, I was there and admiring your great surfing style—bad wave and all!"

They all began firing questions as to whether their mom had been at this place or that, and slowly the family started putting together the missing puzzle pieces of their mom's life and what she had been through. It would take many years to share all the details about her seven years away, but Sarah looked forward to talking about it. She would enjoy the conversations about her hope and how it fed her spirit to survive, knowing that a day like today could happen. They, in turn, were eternally grateful for what she did to protect them and admired her incredible courage under the most dreadful of circumstances.

In the weeks ahead, the family got together many times and shared stories to catch their mom up on the events she had missed out on. These were emotional but mostly joyous times as they recounted when this or that happened, and they loved to watch their mom's reaction, waiting to see if she already knew about it or, if by some chance, had been there to see the event. Each child swore that they had always thought their mom was 'around' and watching over them, but little did they know at the time how close she really was. Only Max and Dr. Kathy had found out about the secret, and both were experts at keeping that secret secure.

To Sarah, Jason finally confessed how he orchestrated the events that led to their escape and who some of the trusted players were that had helped that fateful night.

She was still amazed that his parents had lived next door to her for seven years and not once slipped and told her who the divorced son was. Sarah loved them dearly and felt blessed that they were about to become her in-laws.

Jason loved hearing stories about his wife-to-be and was warmly welcomed by her family. They had lots of questions about his past life and adventures in the FBI. He was almost revered as a superhero to them, and he enjoyed the many questions about his adventures with their mom sneaking around to see them.

Nicholas was present at most of the reunions and encouraged their kids to respect the man who would soon marry their mother. It would have been easy to have been jealous or hurt, but given the situation, Nicholas didn't want to stand in the way of her triumphal return and happiness. He agreed it was *her* turn to enjoy life anew. He admired his once wife and would always have a place in his heart for the mother of his three kids, no matter what, and felt lucky to have married a woman that supported the friendships and shared family times.

Epilogue

On a warm, breezy day, Jason got his wish and married his Sarah on the beach where they first kissed and he proposed, with both sides of their families in attendance. They even included Director Vargas and a handful of FBI agents to share in the joy of the day. The now-elderly Max was carried down the sea cliff to be the ring bearer, with Dr. Kathy as matron of honor and Jason's brother, Jimmy as the best man. Everyone else present was deputized as being part of the small ceremony and in unison gave them both away to each other to forever hold and cherish.

There wasn't a dry eye present that day, and when the new couple left on their honeymoon, no one knew where they were going or when they would be back!

About the Author

Teri Harmon enjoys a successful career as a Financial Planner and Philanthropist involved with projects both locally and overseas. Her lifestyle and activities have exposed her to an amazing cast of real-life characters that have enriched her life and instincts for creative expression and leadership.

Teri is a native Californian, enjoys participating in various games of backgammon, bocce, and cards, loves spending time with her family and friends, and teaches financial literacy to students when not traveling abroad. Teri lives in the Santa Ynez Valley... and just for the record, does not represent the main character in this book!

Teri Harmon
Santa Ynez, CA

CPSIA information can be obtained
at www.ICGtesting.com
Printed in the USA
LVHW051548080722
723063LV00015B/1497